PRAISE FOR
..after..

"Rarely have the effects of any social upheaval been portrayed with such drama and poetic force as in Carolina Rivera Escamilla's book of short pieces about the crisis years in El Salvador. From the shattered hopes and broken lives of the 1980s come these aching stories of memory and loss. With a flair for image and immediacy, Carolina captures her country's recent history as no one has done before—in stories seen through a young girl's eyes, as she lives through dread, trauma and despair until, somehow, in the midst of it all, she finds hope and redemption."
- Marc Zimmerman, author and editor of *Stores of Winter* and nine books on Central American literature.

"With the skills of a poet and a filmmaker, Carolina Rivera Escamilla recreates within these short stories a genuine voice. We are captivated by Dalia's story, as she shows us how to endure and resist oppression. *...after...* should be taught at schools, and hopefully taken to the big screen."
- Alicia Partnoy, author, *The Little School*

"The stories of *...after...*, by Carolina Rivera Escamilla, bring to life with magnificent detail the ideals, the joy, and the drama of survival of the Salvadoran people during crucial moments of their historic and violent past. Here is a fresh and dynamic voice that reminds us that, even during the catastrophe of war, the ideals of art and humanity can guide us to fight for a better world."
-Mario Bencastro, author, *A Shot in the Cathedral*.

Carolina Rivera Escamilla's *After* is the haunting and evocative story of a young woman's political, sexual, and artistic coming of age in the midst of a devastating civil war. By turns gripping

and serene, Escamilla's language is both spare and sensual, reminiscent of Jamaica Kincaid. Shifting time seamlessly, these connected, but self-contained slices of life unfold like delicately etched drawings, telling stories of childhood, womanhood, friendship and family. As readers, we feel the ache of walls of unspoken words between a father and daughter as deeply and sharply as the explosion of a guerilla fighter's grenade. We stir with the questions children have that adults so often leave unanswered as restlessly as those about relatives and friends 'disappeared' by a military government. Like human existence, unimaginable violence and deepest loss exists alongside humor, tenderness, wonder, and always, the hope and hard-fought struggle for a better world.
—Jalondra A. Davis, author of *Butterfly Jar*, lecturer in Africana Studies

"Carolina Rivera Escamilla's stories of the Salvadoran civil war a generation ago read like urgent dispatches from the present--- as they should. A once forbidden history is steadily emerging from the voices of artists back home or far away or somewhere in between. With the unmistakable mark of the great Salvadoran literary tradition from Salarrué to Dalton, and also wearing the bifocals of her diasporic generation, Rivera Escamilla reminds us how far we've come, and how far we have left to go on the Salvadoran road toward la libertad."
—Rubén Martínez, Loyola Marymount University, author of *Desert America: A Journey Across Our Most Divided Landscape*

"In vivid and evocative prose, Carolina Rivera Escamilla captures what it's like to grow up in a country in the midst of civil war, where at any moment a best friend or a family member can disappear. These are moving stories about coming of age in a time of turmoil."
-Mark Jonathan Harris, Writer/director of the Oscar-winning "Into the Arms of Strangers: Stories of the Kindertransport"

...after...

...after...

A COLLECTION OF STORIES BY
CAROLINA RIVERA ESCAMILLA

World Stage Press
Verse from the Village

World Stage Press
Verse from the Village

Copyright © 2015 by World Stage Press
ISBN-13: 978-0-9858659-3-1
ISBN-10: 0985865931

Printed in the United States of America
 Cover Art by Rafael Varela, Salvadoran Painter
 Layout Design by Maximillian Xavier
Cover Design by Lorraine Butler

All characters herein are fictional. Any resemblance to persons, living or dead, is purely coincidental.

This book is dedicated to all my family,
and especially to the memory of my mother.

Acknowledgements

Thanks Mamá, Papá, sisters, brothers, and family for being my source of inspiration all these years as I put together this book. Thank you, husband and son, for encouraging me, even when I disappeared to write for hours, for your support, and for being the ones to read and hear my stories first. Thank you family, mentors, and friends for keeping the encouragement and the story alive. I want to acknowledge the Community Literature Initiative for making this publication happen.

This book is for all humanity and of course for you, dear reader.

Table of Contents

FOREWORD, MANLIO ARGUETA

ALMA ABOUT FOUR-THIRTY IN THE AFTERNOON   1
THE WALL   19
THE RED OLD MAN   25
THE FUNERAL   33
TIME OF THE FATTENED COWS   47
THE BAPTIZED   60
THE KING OF FARTS   64
MACARIO   68
ALTAGRACIA   82
CASAS DE CARTON/ CARDBOARD HOUSES   90
WHEN THE POINTSETTIAS WERE WHITE   100
TERESA- LA SIGUANABA   104
LUCIO MOLINA LINARES   124
THE HUG   130
THE SHORT CUT   136
NIGHT MEMORY   138
THE WHITE-DRESS-UNIFORM-GIRLS   146
LA CARNADA- THE BAIT   152
THE BED   156
AFTER   158

GLOSSARY   175

Foreword

I welcome readily anyone who dares to discover the varied geographies within the fantastic world of literature. The world of the fantastic is not about the great or the phenomenal, but about having created a world from imagination, by making a foray into the unknown where we meet thousands of shapes and feelings. Imagination always takes us on an adventure that seems risky. And risky it is. Imagination (in writing) involves memory and relationships taken from intimate imagery that will have us experience reality, not with mere rationality, but with emotion, dreams, sensitivity and love for others. Imagination is the other reality that tells us who we are, what we love, and what we want for others.

This is what literature expresses by means of the word. So welcome to Carolina Rivera Escamilla's book ...after..., which she has at last delivered to us as a kind of family treasure. When a writer publishes his or her work, it no longer belongs just to her or him, since it has been handed over to its readers. This book is offered to us readers for the taking. Now the feelings of the one who writes turn into the feelings of the one who reads.

This is a book inspired by a family dream--- a girl's dream in which she traces a portrait of brothers and sisters, of a father whose spirit is of well-intentioned deeds for the family. This is especially the portrayal of a mother playing out her eternal role as both morning and evening star, that is to say, a light that for all of her life gives life. And framed thus, also comes the darkness of those who transform hatred into a lamp of dark light, of darkness--- those who ceaselessly persecute those whom they imprison in catacombs, just like ancient Christians. This poetic writer (Rivera Escamilla) also knows all these Salvadoran dramas. She transforms them into an offering for readers, sublimates destructive social details, and transforms them into love letters for her own people and for all readers who accompany her on this journey of life which is writing.

- Manlio Argueta, author A Day of Life, Un día en la vida

…after…

Alma at About Four-Thirty in the Afternoon

I meet my friend Alma at the Art School in San Salvador. She hands me a package. "Be careful. They really need it."

I immediately slide it into my Guatemalan shoulder bag. "What does he look like?" I notice a small opaque gray moth has landed on her right foot. It stands out against the black of her shoe. I remember what my mother says about moths, but I dismiss her superstitions. "He is wearing a beige cotton shirt, faded jeans, has wavy relaxed dark hair, olive-colored skin, and John Lennon style glasses. He's about twenty-five years old. He's handsome, by the way."

"How will he recognize me?"

"I told him you'll be wearing a typical Guatemalan blouse, since you are the only one with that style...very original." She almost breaks into a smile, and then leaves through the gate ahead of me, her face as serious as a cemetery. Her parting words: "Be brave." And from a distance: "Take it easy."

The few times Alma came to my home, she always came with a bag full of vegetables. Once she brought fresh corn from her mother's *milpa*. Sitting at the table, eating lunch with my family, she talked with Mamá about her family and ended up massaging my mother's neck and shoulders. Before going back to art classes, Alma and I would climb the mango tree to gather green mangos. We would cut mangos into thin pieces, and eat them with salt and *chile*. My younger brothers once bet a soda that no one could eat a sour mango with *chile* without making a face. They surround us for one last chance to play with Alma. Alma is sweet with them, always letting them win. She is the champion of making faces when eating the sourest mango.

1

I wait for Alma to be out of sight before I leave with the package. As I catch the bus downtown, I think of the one time I met Alma's mother at the art school.

The nearly forty-year-old woman is standing at the entry gate, carrying a bag in her right hand. She comes inside dressed in an apron with huge pockets in which she carries all her documents and money, like my Aunt Tona. She is taller than Alma and her skin is lighter, but she has the same long black hair and wide clear brown eyes. She seems lost. Her posture shrinks as she takes in the strangeness of boys with long hair—some smoking cigarettes—and girls with jeans shorts and sandals, or '70s style Kicker shoes. Alma, and many of my friends have not been in school for the three days since the students took over the cathedral.

They look so much alike I am sure she is Alma's mother, but I don't approach her until my chemistry teacher, knowing we are friends, asks me to speak with her. "Hi, my name is Dalia. Are you Alma's mother? Alma and I are friends."

"Ay, yes, Alma has talked about you. Are you the one who has a lot of brothers and sisters?" She extends her right hand, after placing her bag on the ground.

"Yes."

"Where's my daughter? Tell me, please, because someone has told me that she is involved in bad things; that she is with these bad men who are giving trouble to the government." Her eyes are wide. "Alma is a good girl. I didn't want to send her here to the capital. This school is crazy. She wants to study music. I want her to get married to a captain in our town, but she doesn't listen to me. She wants to play her violin and be part of the symphony some day." She takes out a white handkerchief and presses it to her wide, wet eyes.

"Come, let's go in," I say. I sit down on the cement ledge at the base of the mural inside the courtyard at the school's entrance. I face the open sky in the direction of the cathedral. She sits next to me as we watch students go by, her body tensing. "I blame her grandfather for insisting she play the violin. He made a violin for her when she was very young, only five years old. They spent hours practicing. She is a good girl. She should have stayed

2

home and married the captain just as her father said before he left us to go work in the city." She blows her nose into her handkerchief. Alma never mentioned the captain to me. Marrying captains, soldiers, and generals is what many parents dream for their daughters, especially in the countryside. My mother and father are not like Alma's parents. They don't even ask if I have a boyfriend.

"Alma is not here, but I'll tell her that you came."

"Where is she? Are you a good girl?"

"She's..." I sigh and look away.

Am I a good girl? What a question to ask. I think of all the cigarettes I smoked with Alma, when I visited her at the occupied cathedral. I think of the two times I smoked pot, the many times I missed school to go to the beach with a painter, a boy older than me. I took off my shirt so he could draw my breasts, then we ended up on the sand kissing each other. Is that what she is asking me? Or does she want to know if I'm also involved in politics?

"Are you a good girl?"

"Yes," I said smiling.

"Where's my daughter? Why isn't she in school? Why don't the teachers punish her for being absent? Why didn't they send me a letter to tell me that she is misbehaving? I can't read, but my younger daughter can read it for me."

I bite my lower lip and pat her on the shoulder. I want to tell her that nobody cares these days about who is present or absent at school. Some teachers are also in the cathedral with Alma. They believe this is part of our education and will not hesitate to give her a grade.

"Tell me where my daughter is. I have to give her this bag. I brought her a new pair of underwear I made for her...and a blouse... some cheese and cream. She doesn't come home on weekends anymore like before." She pats the left side of my lap.

"Alma went to the cathedral on Sunday to pray, and at that moment, students took over the cathedral in a protest about the bad education we are getting," I tell her. "She couldn't get out, but the government will sign the students' petition very soon, and she will be released." She says nothing, so I ask, "Who told you that Alma is involved in bad things?"

3

"Guadalupe… she goes to this school, too. She is studying music like Alma. She plays the piano. She lives next to our house in Concepción."

"Yes, I know her. Don't believe everything she tells you about Alma. She's jealous because Alma has a lot of friends. Everyone likes Alma." I say firmly. Alma's mother is quiet for a moment before asking, "Can you take me to the cathedral?"

"No, no, no one can go there. It is surrounded by soldiers, but she will be fine. She will come out tomorrow and you'll see her then. You can sleep at my house tonight."

"No, I have to go home today. The last bus leaves at three p.m. You know, the bandits stop the buses to rob us as soon as it gets dark. Besides, I can't leave my young children alone. Yesterday my neighbor was killed, and these bandits raped his daughter and wife. People are saying they are *guerrilleros* against the government, but I am not sure they are right. I don't know what is happening anymore, because suddenly we are seeing these banditos, but we are also seeing men we know are good people who also are covering their faces and heads." She puts her hands inside her apron pockets.

"So it is better for you to go to the terminal to catch your bus. I'll tell Alma to go home this weekend. She will be happy to know that you came to see her. Let's go. I'll walk you to the bus stop." I am already on my feet heading toward the gate. I look up at the sky and notice clouds are building up into a dark gray.

"Please give my daughter this bag. Take care of her. She told me you're a good friend to her, and she knows your family. Don't let my daughter get involved in bad things. Tell her to come home, but not after dark because the bandits are killing people, no matter who they are." She puts her handkerchief inside one of the wide apron pockets, hands me the bag, and shakes my hand to say goodbye.

In her I see my mother and the everyday worry in this country for the security of daughters and sons. I think the mothers of the poor suffer most because their children have been the first to join the struggle to fight the government for improvements in their lives and for those of the generations that will follow us. "I'll take care of her. I'll come with Alma to visit you this weekend."

4

I wave goodbye to her at the bus stop. She waves to me from the bus.

I never went to visit Alma's mother, and Alma never went back to her house. It is dangerous for her now, because Guadalupe's family found out about Alma's involvement with the guerrillas. Guadalupe married the captain who was supposed to marry Alma. Alma's mother tells the entire village that bandits killed Alma when she was coming home to see her, but Alma did see her mother once more. They met secretly at the village church.

Alma came disguised as a city woman in a wavy brunette wig. She wore heavy make-up, a stylish dress, and high-heeled shoes. Later she told me it's almost impossible to walk in high-heeled shoes. A man accompanied her. Nobody recognized her, not even her mother, not until she sat down next to her, pinched her mom's elbow and smiled. They went to the rear of the church. That day Alma told her mother that it was good she told the neighbors in the village that the bandits had killed her. "You'll be safer now, and my little sisters, too." They hugged, they cried, and too soon the Mass was finished. Alma had caused her mother to miss Mass.

When people ask me about Alma, I have to say I don't see her much anymore. I don't explain that we are both involved in the country's political situation: I, in political theater performances, and she, in the mountains with the guerillas. We seldom find time to talk anymore, especially about ourselves, as we did so often in earlier days.

I leave the school and walk along the boulevard to the bus stop. There are soldiers everywhere. Some of the soldiers stop people and ask for their documents. Mostly, they stop young students like me. The package is heavy. I feel my right shoulder dropping lower and starting to go numb. I try to focus straight ahead on the street, but my lips and eyes will not stay still, as I aim toward the arriving bus.

Shit. God, whoever you are, and wherever you are, under the earth or above the clouds, listen to me now. I'm sorry I've denied you so many times, just as your disciple Pedro did, but you have got to understand that with all the misery and killing going on here, it's easier to befriend the devil than to be a friend of yours. Look, even priests have been killed, but today, do me this favor, make me invisible, or make the package in my bag light and... Shit. How can I ask you this now, if I have never been a believer? I know that if the soldiers stop me now, if they open the package, it will be over. Yes, my life, my little life will be over. On bus twenty-two, I hold the heavy shoulder bag package on my lap on my way to downtown.

Alma and I entered Art School the same year. We had both just turned sixteen, fresh young students starting high school. As I got close to the school, on my first day there, my breathing ran fast and heavy like a river after a big storm. I had gone through the auditions two weeks earlier, and I felt so proud of having passed them and for having been accepted into El Centro Nacional de Bellas Artes. My oldest brother was delighted.

Mamá and Papá were not quite convinced I should study theater. "You should go to sewing school," my mother told me. "Look, Milagro is already working in the factory, and is a seamstress at home for many people in the *colonia*." When she says this, my mother is seated at the kitchen table, a pile of my brothers' and father's pants at her feet. She mends them one by one. I guess she says this in case I want encouragement or permission to change my mind about theater. I slip through the curtain into my room, pretending to look for something to write with. Then, I return to the main room of the house.

My father says, "Well, you're going to be an actress now. Next thing you know, we'll see you on Mexican soap operas." "No, that's a load of crap," I say, sounding very much like him. "I hope one day I can go to Russia to study theater and the methods of Stanislavsky and Bertolt Brecht." In fact, I don't know anything about these big names. At school, I heard that some new teachers who had been in Russia are coming to teach us the methods of Brecht and Stanislavsky. "What did you say?" Papá puts some Vaseline in his hair, combing it back with the same black comb he sometimes uses as a harmonica. "Ah, nothing," I answer. "Russia!" he yells. I run into my room fast. I want to put on my only pair of Levi jeans and sandals to go out. He pushes aside the brown polyurethane curtain that serves as the door between the bedroom I share with my two sisters and the living room. Holding his black comb in his right hand, punctuating his words, he says, "Be careful what you say. Right now you could be killed in this country just for mentioning that place." I laugh nervously. He leaves murmuring, "She wants to be a communist. Well, at least she's not foolish... she's growing up." As I leave to go to school, I say "Bye, see you at supper," and my father hands me two *colones*. "Thank you," I whisper.

On that first day, walking through the entrance of the Art School, I see Alma, leaning against the huge Dalí-esque mural just inside the main gate. Over the center of the mural, someone has painted the huge figure of a camouflaged soldier with an M-3 rifle. Alma leans against the wall right where the point of the rifle barrel ends. It is still early, so I wait, leaning against the mural too.

Her arms are crossed. It occurs to me that people with arms folded don't want to be bothered by anyone. I keep observing her. Perhaps she is just shy. My sister does that when she is uncertain, but once she knows you, you can't contain her. When Alma is not looking, I scrutinize her from toe to head. I suspect she is doing the same thing to me, but when I look toward her face, she is looking at my feet. I like her very long straight black hair. She starts playing with it, rolling it around her finger. I've always wanted long hair, but my mother complains that my hair gets full of lice, so she never lets me grow it.

Alma moves closer to me, still looking at my feet. I finally figure out why. My sandals and hers are exactly the same. Brown leather, with straps and thick soles cut from old tires. I move closer to her, too.

"Where did you buy your sandals? Are you new here? What's your name?" She is right in front of me, with her smile and child's eyes, pointing at my feet. "My father makes them," she says. "You must have bought yours at Mercado Cuartel. That's the only place that sells them." "Yes, you're right," I say, and that's all it takes to start our friendship.

We walk to class and discover we have the same morning classes. I sit next to her, and she tells me she passed the audition for music. She has her violin with her. At noon I invite her to eat lunch at my house, but she says she brought food with her and prefers to stay at the school. She has mentioned she's from the countryside, and I sense the city is new for her. I stay with her, waiting for our afternoon classes. I do not want to go home anyway.

I haven't missed lunch at home for sixteen years, and I picture all my brothers and sisters in line waiting for Mamá to fill their plates. Nobody eats twice in my house so Mamá will save my plate of food for later. I hope she doesn't come to look for me at school.

We sit under a mango tree behind the classroom, the thin dark green leaves dressing the brown branches. Alma opens a plastic bag and brings out a hard square of cheese, a small roll of French bread, and a container of cooked red beans. "Let's eat," she says. I like the cheese.

For a few months during the two free hours we have everyday before afternoon classes start, Alma plays her violin while I dance around the mango tree. We laugh so hard whenever she dances while I try to play her violin. Together, Alma and I are magic, and our magic helps us to forget the daily routine. "Do you think we will always stay close friends?" we ask each other.

"I want to bring you to the green hills, near where I live," she says, showing me a book of stories she has written about the green hills of Amatepec, just outside the capital, where during the week she rents a room in a house.

"When? Tomorrow? Let's not go to school." I'm eager to escape the daily presence of soldiers at school trying to intimidate our teachers and interrogate us. "Anyway, we don't even have classes really," I add to convince myself more than Alma.

"Let's do it! We'll meet tomorrow at *el parque* Libertad." Alma nods her head and grins. She heads toward her music class humming Beethoven's Fifth Symphony.

"I'll read you the monologue I'm working on," I yell to her, but I regret my words as soon as they leave my mouth. My monologue is stupid. It is about all kinds of insects living in peace in a community. I hope she doesn't laugh. The protagonist is a frog that talks to ants and a butterfly. I'll explain that it is an analogy assignment from my drama class---which is true.

Otherwise, I would not be writing about bugs. At any rate, my handwriting is terrible, like a hen with ink on her beak trying to scribble on the ground. Alma writes beautifully, but she puts Vs for Bs and vice versa, and disregards accent marks. We're the same that way. I'll read her the monologue.

I arrive at *el parque* Libertad at nine in the morning. Alma is buying a bag of sliced mangos with chili from a vendor in the park. I walk slowly behind her, tuck my index finger into her back like a gun, and say, "Documents out, young woman." "Hey, you scared me." She turns around to face me. "I was imagining some illiterate soldiers asking me for my papers." The woman with the basket of mangos offers a nervous but friendly smile, and sells me another bag of mangos. "There's the bus!" She indicates the opposite corner of *el parque*. We jump on the bus and off we go.

The place is only about twenty minutes away from the city center. The road is still paved where we get off the bus, and Alma leads me up the dirt road that begins a few steps away. After a few hundred meters on the dirt road we head into the bushes. Alma moves aside some bamboo branches. "Over there, can you see the tall trees and the green of the hills?" The hills are a faraway wall meeting the infinite blue sky. The ripe yellow sun dissolves onto the green grass. There are a few short guava trees in the middle of the grassy area, and bamboo takes over its edges. There are no birds singing here, only Alma and I who run downward in a sloping spiral into the infinite green hills.

"Let's go there." I point to a spot in the distance. "I want to lie down on the little patch of green grass." I smile at Alma. We find a spring. I jump over it, turn quickly, and splash Alma in the face, just as she bends down close to the creek to throw water at me.

"Let's see who is the more thirsty one here," she says, coming at me with water cupped in her hands.

"See if you can rain on me. I am the earth." I yell and act out the role of the earth, arms uplifted in a graceful and silly pose.

"I am the rain. I will soak you, Earth! Rain, rain, drop your rain over her face," she sings, as she sprinkles water all over herself, and on me, too. We kneel again with arms uplifted to the sky. I imagine a great public audience watching me from the sky.

"Let's act out the monologue you need to practice for your exam." She sits down on the grass.

"I forgot to bring it. The actor has to talk and move like an animal. I'm going to be a frog that talks to ants and butterflies. The frog helps the ants, worms, and snakes, and he shows them how to live in peace, and to share. It's stupid!" Alma jumps around the grass like a frog. She hides behind a bush. I extend my arms and pretend I am a butterfly floating up and down the hill. The frog comes to me and says, "Butterfly, butterfly, let's go catch bugs to feed the poor." I laugh. We laugh. I fall to the ground laughing and hold my stomach, I am laughing so hard. Alma falls onto her back laughing, too.

Trying to catch our breath, I suggest an exercise I learned in voice class, one of Chekov's theater techniques. "Get up and stand straight. Bend from your waist until your head touches your knees. Take a big breath and hold it." I stop to open my notebook and find the page with the exercise so I can guide Alma better. "Imagine that you're becoming small, like a coiled spring. Draw yourself in. Contract, and shrink, as though your body and your spirit will disappear within yourself. The space around you is reduced to air." I see Alma shrinking into a position like a snail on the grass. "Let your breath go and let out a scream to expand all your body." Alma explodes into laughter.

I run to the other side of the knoll and lie down to let the sun dry me. Alma is laughing as she follows me. With her face to the sun she spins in circles yelling, "I feel free, free!" and ends up at my side laughing. I read some of her stories. She allows me to keep them "forever, if you want." The thin copybook with a cheap cover is like the ones my mother buys for my brothers who are in elementary school. "Is your stomach making noises?" I ask her. "Yeah, I am hungry. I want to eat." She looks down, and hears another growl. "Listen to my crying belly." We return to downtown around three in the afternoon, wet, hungry, and still laughing.

After eight months at the Art School, however, things have changed. The soldiers sack the school, searching for weapons that aren't there. They smash all the art supplies. They smear and spill paint everywhere in the theatre rooms and ask why there is so much red paint at this school. They smash the mirrors in the make-up room. They break all the furniture. The soldiers pick up students, who then disappear, their bodies never found. Others flee northward. The chemistry teacher is killed at a teachers' protest. Thousands of students fill the streets in daily protests. They shout for better education and justice for the poor. Students take over the cathedral. The police and armed forces' trucks circle the church shooting at the students. Once in a while, other students throw bags of food from passing buses, but quickly pull their arms back inside, before they can be caught. People walk nervously and everyone is scared when they see soldiers motioning with their rifles.

I know the plan: I have to get off bus number twenty-two, at the cathedral. Then, I will walk to *el parque* Libertad to catch bus number twenty-seven to the university. I hope I don't see anyone I know. There is always something going on at the cathedral. If there is no Mass, there will be a protest taking place. Also, el Teatro Nacional is close by. I don't want to see anyone I know.
Just before the students took the cathedral, Alma became directly and fully involved in the guerilla movement. I got more involved in politics, too, but only through art. I perform in political theatre in the city plazas and parks, at the national markets and in public schools in the countryside. One day before a performance of "Super Pancho" in El Mercado de San Miguelito, Super Pancho, the main character of the play, who is played by my secret boyfriend, directs my attention to a guy in the audience. Super Pancho is our theatre teacher and the director of the group.
"Who's that guy?" I ask while I work the whiteface make-up onto Super Pancho's face. He waits for me to finish his lips with a black liner and says, "He works with Alma. He performs puppets in Guazapa. He's in charge of the shows for the *compañeros* in the Cerro de Guazapa."
"I didn't know they had theatre there. How does he know Alma?" I change my costume to become my role, the Bruja Caluja. My character is supposed to represent the government that steals candies and food from the children.
"She is there in Guazapa. They work together. Send a letter to Alma with him. He knows her very well." It crosses my mind

11

that this might be her boyfriend, the guy she told me she liked. I start writing a letter, but my secret boyfriend tells me, "Hurry up and change, because we need to practice the new lines. Write the letter after the show. He'll be staying to talk to us. They might want us to come to Guazapa to perform." I set the square mirror before me to put on my make-up. He places the witch's hat on my head. Then I help Lucía put on her make-up, too. Lucía is the third person in our group. She plays Comin Comion, a stupid, ignorant, innocent guy who does everything La Bruja Caluja tells him to do. I hear the noises of the children and their mothers waiting for the performance. The mothers are the market sellers and their young children stay with them to help them sell.

Before I start writing, my secret-boyfriend tells me, "Don't write her real name in the letter."

I frown at him, "I know that. And I know her clandestine name."

Hi, Tania,

I am writing this note from el Mercado San Miguelito. I met the guy who does puppetry there where you are. My boyfriend, Santos, knows him very well. Today is the fourth performance we've done in the markets. We've not yet gone to the schools to perform, because my boyfriend says it is hard to convince directors of the schools to let us perform our piece. I am playing a witch who steals the poor children's food and candy. In the end, Super Pancho and the children capture the witch and put her in jail. We let the children decide what they want to do with the witch and they always want to send her to work. Super Pancho tells them that the witch doesn't have any skills, because all her life she has stolen from the poor. The children are willing to teach her carpentry and other jobs. One boy stood up and came to the stage to say that he will teach her to be Batman and Superman because they are good heroes and they don't steal. The audience laughed. Well, the puppet guy can tell you more about today's presentation.

I miss you a lot. Mamá and my little brothers ask for you almost everyday. Take care.

Caluja.

"Come on, he has to go." Super Pancho approaches me on the improvised backstage where we have all the props for the performance. "I'll be ready in a moment." I rip the page from my notebook, fold it and hand it to the puppet guy. He takes it and smiles at me. "Good play, good acting too. I'll tell Alma." He moves through the people from the market. He is a lean shadow disappearing into the crowd. I walk back to the improvised stage where Lucia and Super Pancho are gathering the props. Super Pancho throws me the witch hat, suggesting with his look that I should be careful with it. I have already lost the hat a few times and he always gets mad. But he still makes me a new one. The last time I lost it, a kid stole it and ran away. I saw him do it, and let it go. They need to play. They don't have toys. The hat is quite fancy with fake gold and silver *chiclet* coins all around it. That's why the children want it.

I pack my stuff and wait for Lucía to step out of the miniature backstage area. I throw myself against my secret boyfriend's chest and kiss his lips even though they still have gray lip liner. He kisses me for a long moment and says, "Let's go. I have to pick up my daughter, and the dogs are here already." I see soldiers entering the market as we exit.

When I see el Teatro Nacional and the Cathedral, it's time for me to get off bus twenty-two. The indigenous faces of soldiers, boys my age from the countryside or the *rancherías* around the capital, are stationed at the corners around the cathedral. The huge red Coca-Cola billboard next to the cathedral steps reminds me who really controls our country. I walk the two blocks to *el parque* Libertad at a normal pace and I board bus number twenty-seven to the university.

Once Alma and I worked together on a bus. "Hurry up! Let's get on the bus for Soyapango!" I get a seat in the front of the bus; she finds a seat towards the middle. I open up a newspaper and read aloud for all to hear. "Yesterday the guerillas attacked two military headquarters."

From the middle of the crowded bus, Alma calls, "Which ones?"

13

"El Zapote y Santa Ana." I answer like a news anchor on the television news.

"How many military were killed?"

"Let me see..." I scan the newspaper..."forty-one militaries killed by the guerillas." Although I read this aloud, something strange happens to my voice. It comes out hollow and bitter like a sad memory stuck in knots between my throat and my chest. In that short moment I think about Dora surrounded by military and shot to death in *el parque* Cuscatlán---and of Trompita, the musician, his body burned and disappeared by chemicals, a favored military tactic to horrify the people. His green eyes are the only things I can remember, the only part of his body said to be found on the road. Then that dark night when Carlos and his girlfriend were taken away from their homes and we never saw them again. Stories circulate about all the peasants killed in the mountains by the military forces. But the moment passes and calls me back to my task, which is to spread the word that the guerrillas are luminous, alive and fighting in the mountains. Although the front page of the newspaper says that more civilians and *guerilleros* have been killed than military, I only tell the people about the military deaths.

We both stand up and distribute pamphlets and propaganda– something these people would never voluntarily pick up–to the passengers. We keep our eyes on the windows, making sure there are no soldiers in the distance. All day long, changing from bus to bus, we get the message out like this. As we step off the bus, Alma's left fist shoots into the air as she shouts, *"¡Patria, o muerte, venceremos!"*

The second time we work together is close to the art school. It is about three o'clock in the afternoon, and we are on our way back with some *compañeros* from a *MERS* protest in front of the American Embassy. Alma and I do some graffiti on a neighborhood wall that reads: *MERS: Movimiento Estudiantil Revolucionario de Secundaria is alive and present in the struggle!* Alma steps back from the long brick wall to appreciate the red and black graffiti. I am still squatting with the can in my right hand finishing the last words, but I can sense her behind me in her khaki MacArthur pants, her plaid boy's shirt with its four buttons. She has a hat on her head. We look the same, only my

14

pants are faded Levis. We cross the street in the direction of the art school. Once inside the school, we will drop off the spray cans and discuss the protest.

Two blocks away from school, we hear an explosion and a ball of smoke rises from the direction of the school. We rush to the corner to see a firebombed red truck. "It's better we stay away," I suggest.

"I just hope that Conchita's restaurant didn't get blown away." Alma says, putting a hand in her pants pocket. The sweet smoky stench of burnt Coca Cola stays with us all the way to the bus stop. We decide to walk all the way to *el parque* Libertad.

Soon I will be at the university. Bus twenty-seven is passing through El Estado Mayor, the Military School, where the green-painted buildings, trucks and uniforms have given me goose bumps ever since I walked here with Mamá when I was little to see my aunt who lived in a nearby *colonia* bordered by *rancherías*.

Before today, the last time Alma and I worked together was probably more than six months ago. It began at a meeting where some *compañeros* informed us about the new American buses arriving in the country. The buses were being sensationalized on the radio and television news. "The American President Ronald Reagan is helping our society by sending new technology," our newscasters told us in their most soothing voices. They said, "the new buses have both radio and television... they are very nice."

Alma stands up. "Reagan is taking us for idiots. He's trying to be funny by sending the buses as a cover for the military weaponry he is secretly sending."

The next day when the buses are put into service, almost all of them are firebombed. They are "very nice" but they do not really have radios and televisions inside. After Alma and I empty all the passengers out of one bus, Alma postures herself like an eagle ready to fly, and, facing north with a grenade in her hand, she yells angrily, "Reagan, American Imperialists, we shit on your brains and stick your dreams of technological superiority up your ass! Don't you remember Vietnam?"

15

While she talks, I go back to gather up any forgotten bags or belongings to reunite them with the passengers outside. We warn them to run away. As we set fire to the last bus of the day, we hear, and then see, tanks approaching in the distance. After Alma has made sure I am out of the bus, she pulls the pin of a grenade and lets it fly through the open door of the bus. We run in different directions, losing ourselves in the crowds. That was the last time I was with her before receiving this package from her today.

I finally arrive at the Universidad Simeon Cañas at about a quarter to six. I rendezvous in the social sciences department, on the shady corner that has an exit from the campus, at the exact place Alma described. I find the man in the beige cotton shirt and faded jeans, just as she said I would. We've just met when the shockwave and heat of an explosion turns us both involuntarily in a direction about a block away. We see chaos, students running, trying to escape as soldiers move in quickly through smoke, striking students, aiming and shooting their guns at them.

The young man tears the shoulder bag from my arm, squats, pulls the package from the bag, rips it open, and hands me a 38-caliber pistol. He scoops up all the other weapons for himself, telling me to move. "Do you know how to use it?" he asks, wiping the sweat from his forehead with his left hand. Suddenly, intensely, I feel the same wave of humidity and heat. He looks for an exit. I want to say, "It's hot," but instead I say, "Right, yes, I've had some lessons."

He removes his glasses and I look at his eyes. They are hazel set in a heart-shaped face. He takes the corner of his beige cotton shirt and wipes his glasses. I want to tell him to wipe the sweat from around his eyes. But I just watch him move. I squat leaning my back into the wall to be at his level. He seems to appreciate my move and draws close to my face and whispers that the attack in El Zapote hasn't gone well. "They surrounded the *compañeros* before they could attack. Alma was the leader of the mission. They killed everyone."

I run out of the university, crying, tucking the weapon inside my jeans. Which of these filthy fucking soldiers killed Alma?

Why did she have to die, and why should I have to kill? I slow down to walk calmly through the long messy traffic-filled Calle Panamericana. I have to act normal so nobody suspects my pain. I think about my mother, wiping her eyes as she leaves her bedroom. I ask, "What's wrong, Mamá?" but only later learn my two cousins had been killed. "Nothing, keep going. Don't show what you feel; it can be dangerous," I sense my mother saying, straightening up, smiling. Is she smiling? Yes, she is. It helps me to continue. I cross to the other side of the street without noticing the light signal. I can't distinguish whether it is red, green, yellow or white. The soldiers stare at me. It is starting to rain. I can feel the drops on my face, and I see the windshield wipers on the cars and buses flipping back and forth. Then everything blurs.

It is nine o'clock, and I'm finally at home. I go to the bedroom. My sisters are sleeping. Everyone is sleeping, except Mamá. She doesn't ask me anything. I've already put the pistol under the mattress. I listen to my sisters' breathing, --- dolls full of dreams. I cannot sleep. I am afraid someone may have followed me. I look at the corrugated metal wall. Soldiers sometimes pass through the property along the other side and scrape the metal wall with their rifles. I hate that sound.

I cannot tell anyone that Alma is dead. If my Mom finds out, I will not be allowed to return to school. I worry that someone in the *colonia* saw me at the university today. This *colonia* has many *orejas*.

Nata, the owner of the local store, calls to the people in the *colonia* that the French rolls have arrived and are still warm. It is six o'clock in the morning. I have not slept. I go outside to get water from the cement laundry sink. I scoop water with my hands and splash it on my face. It is cold and smells like spring water, even though it is almost October, near the end of the rainy season. The cold of the water reminds me of the time I played with Alma in the hills. I look up at the long green mango leaves dangling and moving in the wind. The sun's rays are filtered through the tree branches to the wet ground where I stand. They shine on the mango tree's trunk. A tiny salamander looks for its way up the tree.

17

"What are you looking at there, wasting your time? You should have started the fire for the coffee on the woodstove an hour ago." It's my mother's voice.

"There's a baby salamander on the tree." I do not face my mother.

"Ah, I know, your father found the mother and its babies on the avocado tree and put them in that hole in the mango tree. I think they were just born a few days ago."

I wish she hadn't told me the story of the salamanders. I want to think that it is Alma entering the world in a new shape. Alma told me once that when she died, she wanted to be an animal in her new life. I told Alma I wanted to be a spider to weave the world the way I wanted it.

"Like Spiderman, in the comic books," she laughs.

"No, like Spiderwoman who saves the red star. Spiderman is a capitalist, the USA's secret missionary, always helping others at no cost." Alma laughs and gestures with her fingers to put quotation marks around the word "cost." We laugh.

Mamá is waiting for me at the table, by the time I am ready for school. She made a pot of coffee. There is a plastic cup of coffee on the table, accompanied by a French roll. I come to sit with her.

"Why are you so quiet this morning? What's wrong with your eyes? What is the matter with you?" "Nothing." I turn my face from her.

"Did you hear that El Zapote was attacked? Many *muchachos* were killed."

"Yes, and a girl, too."

The Wall

I like the brick wall, the one Papá built of brick. The other ones are made of corrugated metal like at Cande's, my friend's house, although mine are shiny and new, while hers are rusty and decaying with holes. My little brothers yell to her from the street, "Your house is a colander," and Cande hurls at them the first stone she finds on her patio, stones with dry fallen coffee tree leaves stuck to them. Her house is inside a coffee grove. Mine is on the edge of a gully. I always defend Cande. I invite her in the afternoons to touch the brick wall and to play TIC TAC TOE on it.

One night Papá tells us he built the brick wall from bricks left over from the last mansion he finished in the neighborhood of Escalón. People from my neighborhood, my girlfriends, my sisters, and brothers get jealous of me, because I love my wall. They tell me that I nurture that wall like I do our baby sister, the baby of the house. To my baby sister I give kisses all over her little face, as I comb her fine hair. Before Christmas arrives, my brothers, sisters and I remove everything from the wall in order to paint it. My sister Estela and I, as the older ones, get to give orders to the little ones. My older brothers do not want to paint the wall anymore with us. They say that is a game for kids, not for them. They exit the house wearing their bellbottom pants. The oldest takes his guitar and both have their long hair covering their faces. When I go out to see where they are going, they have already joined his friends who are parked on a corner of the street.

Nevertheless, today, it is they who blended the whitewash for us, before they went to work with Papá. They mixed it in a barrel that they themselves cut to adjust it lower to our size, so we could reach the barrel's bottom with our rough brushes. Angel, the eldest, had already drawn a blue window with clouds that look like mice under an orange sun on the outside of the wall, and he tells us, "Do not even try to paint anything or even touch the exterior wall. Don't even look at the wall on the

19

outside. Stay inside to paint. I'm working on a mural outside."
We all peek at the outside wall as soon as Angel is out of sight.

On the inside wall usually hang the most important family objects. So, three days before Christmas, my sister and I take down: the calendars that the store lady, Nata, gave us last Christmas; a poster of *El Divino Salvador del Mundo*; a fake stone necklace that hangs from a rusted nail; and the two felt-covered pieces of soda cork covered with a purple and red velvet my sister and I made as our gifts last Mothers' Day. Mine has the shape of a vine with grapes, and my sister's is shaped like a strawberry. When I take these last two down from among all the other Mothers' Day gifts, I sneeze as a layer of fine dust fans out into the space. We all laugh because Javier, the youngest of us, tries to grab the dust sparkles to save them in his pants' pocket. The gifts from my little brothers are all color-pencil drawings inside heart-shaped construction paper.

Estela is in charge of taking down the photographs of my great-grandmother, my grandmother, my mother and father's portraits from when they were twenty and twenty seven years old, and photos of my older brothers. In reality, seven of the photos are very fine drawings in pencil, drawn by an artist friend of my oldest brother. One day Angel's friend visited us, and Mamá gave him some *colones* and the seven oxidizing photos. One month later, Angel's friend delivered the yellow-brown photos and their drawings that looked exactly like the photos, except new. Mamá had them framed in black and white frames with glass. The portraits show more emotions and feelings within their beautiful black and brown eyes than the original pictures. We hang them on the wall. Any important thing has to go on the brick wall.

My little brothers line up along the wall to splash cups of water on it. Then we give each a soapy rag to wipe the wall as hard as they can. After that they dry it with pieces of cloth they each find by themselves inside various places in the house. My brother Antonio, Junior, is in charge of pulling nails from the wall. He likes that job because he can use Papá's hammer that he hangs on his belt just like Papá.

I always invite Cande to help us paint the wall, and if there is some paint left, we haul the barrel over to her house to paint the corrugated metal walls on the inside of her house. Last time we painted, the whitewash did not go very well, as the paint did not stay white, as it dissolved into a color not unlike Mamá's old photos. My brother Angel says old photos were sepia in color, but I think it's just yellow-brown, although sepia sounds prettier. Nevertheless, Cande said that it does not matter; the walls look better urine yellow than sooty black from the oven and rusty brown from all the leaks.

With Estela we finally bring over the barrel filled with whitewash to our wall. This year Cande is not here. The four brushes made from *mezcal* look like horses' tails and are already in my little brothers' hands. When the barrel comes, they all come at once to the barrel, surround it, but before they can submerge the brushes, we interrupt them and tell them to put the brushes on the floor. Their happy sunflower faces shift immediately into withering flowers, as they bend down their heads and place the four brushes on the floor. After a brief silence, I explain to them that Estela and I will paint the top part of the wall. I pick up two of the brushes. "Do not get too close to us as we paint up high, because if the whitewash splatters and falls on your face, you could go blind, and if it falls on your skin, you might disappear." I tell them this, and all seven of them move away from us. Estela tells five of them, "Go out to play now." They obediently disappear out the door. She moves the other two side-by-side a little away from the wall. I call Antonio, Jr. and Javier to stay there with us. I take Antonio, and my sister takes Javier. She stands Javier on a chair facing the wall. "Close your eyes, you have to paint with your senses." Javier takes the paintbrush, and before his brush can touch the wall, whitewash somehow splatters onto his face. We take him down fast from the chair and carry him to the barrel under the mango tree. The big barrel is full of water from the last two months' storms. We throw two buckets full of water on him, and he starts screaming, "I can't see, I can't see, the white wash has left me blind." We laugh. The other children and even a few neighbors have all come out alarmed and startled by Javier's screams.

Before we can get back to our task, Estela changes Javier out of his wet clothes and puts him to bed, adding a bit of drama by covering his eyes with a piece of cloth. The traumatized Javier falls asleep. Estela, Antonio, Jr., and I finish painting the wall. My little brothers and little sister help us after the wall is dry with pieces of cloth, as we show them how to do touch-ups on the wall. As they sponge the wall with dry patches of cloth, they remind me of how Mamá would dip clean cloth into beans and soups to feed us tastes of food when we were babies. Now my brothers feed the wall as once we were fed. Mamá and Papá have arrived home near sunset, and they congratulate us for the work on the wall. The wall looks wider, and I imagine it like a sea. In an instant, it transforms itself into a desert with short pathways. The wall is the bed I dream of having there against it. It becomes a canoe and takes me to the other side of the world, perhaps China. I weave myself into the wall, and now both the wall and I become a warm blanket that covers the roof of this little house, while my brothers and sisters and parents sleep. Mamá tells us it is time to get ready to go to bed in our sleeping areas. Papá tells us that later he will give some extra brushing to the wall to even out the white color.

Since the sun is already set, the night looks divided to me between the stark light that reflects from the living room wall and the dull light reflected in all the corrugated metal walls. I imagine the wall is a purple moon. I sit on top of it to see all the world's Christmas trees. If I had had other paint colors, I would have painted it the color of a late red afternoon over a baby blue sky with horizons in violet, purple, yellow, even green. And there would be Estela and my brothers and I playing hopscotch. But we only have whitewash, because real paint is too expensive, and Papá and Mamá do not have money to buy colored paint. Yet I have seen my wall painted like a sunset in my dreams. I wash up and go to bed.

Late at night, when everyone is knocked out, or dizzy, as my Papá says, I get up to examine the wall. She does not want to go to sleep either, and so I join the wall as we illuminate the silence of the night. I kneel and contemplate her, as though she is my patron saint, or the witch who will work miracles for me. I like her eyes. I am the only one who knows where they are, since I invented them for her. They are watermelon seeds on a cotton tablecloth, and her sunflower eyelashes cover me when I hear the neighborhood dogs start barking. The paint is nearly dry, so I softly run my fingers over her, carefully plucking the mescal hairs that stayed on her while we were painting. The removed hairs leave their prints that look like skinny drunk serpents that do not know where are they going. The snaky prints are veins in her white body. From a distance in the living room, I observe now the white brick wall and see it like a child's baptismal gown boxed among the other three corrugated dull metal walls. Christmas always finds our brick wall ready to be dressed again in new jewelry, school gifts, as she readies to play with friends like Cande and to trace out the New Year.

…after…CAROLINA RIVERA ESCAMILLA

The Red Old Man

"You didn't go to school today?" Nata comes out to the street, looking like a pale inflated balloon with tarantula legs and arms. People bark at you if you miss school in this *colonia*.

"No, I left my uniform outside last night. It got very wet." I look down at the dirty water, only half paying attention to Nata's legs in white stockings close to the puddle.

"Why didn't you iron it, lazy little girl?"

"Our iron is not electric like yours," I answer her. "It needs a lot of wood coals." I jump into the puddle, making sure to splash the brown water all over her. "Oh, oh you little devil. I hope very soon, the red old man scares you, when you become a woman!" She screams this at me, so that other women going to market can hear her and call my mother. I run inside my house before Mamá can come to hit me with a stick.

Doña Nata, whenever she encounters the neighborhood women either on their way to or from the bus stop at the end of our street, moves alongside my mother whenever she joins the group to shop at El Mercado Central. Then Nata stands in front of Mamá, holds her own hands together behind her back, her stomach extending as big as a watermelon, even though she is not pregnant. She says, "Oh, your daughter's breasts are starting to show! Don't let her wear tight T- shirts. I have seen the men's eyes narrow and their shoulders widen when she passes in front of them. Has the red old man visited her yet?" My mother only listens to her because she lets her buy food for the family on credit at her tiny market in her living room. We always pay later.

I go inside the house. I stand on top of a chair trying to reach the window to see whether the women have gone by yet. The silence of the morning grows in my feet. I sit down on the metal chair and little by little I give sound to the silence, smacking my bare feet on the tile floor as I look in at Mamá's room.

She stares into the tiny broken mirror she grips in her hand as she combs her long black hair with her fingers, touches her

25

cheeks, examines her mouth and the empty spaces where her molars used to be. The mirror with the big crack down the middle of it divides her thirty-eight-year-old face. We girls never use a mirror. Everybody else's eyes tell us how we look. The broken mirror used to belong to my cousin, Teresa. She picks up things the rich people leave next to the trash cans on the street.

"Mamí, why don't you buy a mirror?" I move aside the curtain that separates her room from the living room, sitting down on her bed.

"You and your brothers and sisters break them." She moves quickly out of the room to join my aunts in the kitchen. I want to ask her about the red old man, but instead I follow and sit at a distance from the women. The morning is moving quickly. The clear yellow light has already hit the mango tree's branches. Aunt Lina is visiting us today. We used to live in her house, but she married an evangelic man who told her to sell the house and to kick us out.

I come back inside to my oval chair, move it close to the radio and put on some music. "Dalia, turn off the radio and start cleaning the house, and then wash the dishes," Mamá yells from the kitchen. The kitchen looks more like an improvised patio. From there you can see all the neighbors going by to Nata's store, or heading to get to bus number five. We always have to say "goodbye," or "how are you?" to passersby. We ignore the ones we specifically don't like or don't know by running inside the house. The people always turn their heads to look at our kitchen. Papá should have walled it in all around.

"I already swept the floor, Mamí. Washing dishes... it's not my turn today." I turn down the radio. My aunts stand talking in the kitchen doorway. Their faces lean in closely to one another. They are both tiny women, small feet shifting in sandals and flat black shoes. Their little hands move in different directions as they talk. Sometimes they glance at me accusingly, as though I am trying to steal their thoughts.

My curly-haired aunt, her name is Margarita, but we children like to call her Tía Yita. I like her curly hair, and she is the only one with curly hair. Mamá says it's because she has a different father from hers, but that's never been a problem, since they love each other as though they have the same father. None of their fathers were around anyway; only my grandmother was there for them. My Tía Yita and her two children live with us. Tía Yita never sits in a chair to eat with us or to talk. She is always standing. If I ask her to sit, she answers scratching her head that she has no time to waste.

"It is a problem to have daughters," Aunt Lina says from nowhere. Perhaps she is picking up a conversation left hanging from the last time she visited. "You never know where they are going to end up," my curly-haired aunt says with a shy expression on her face, as she looks in my direction. I pretend I am listening to the radio and not to them.

"What are you listening to?" Aunt Lina comes close to me and touches my hair. "It's a song in English. It says 'plise, plise don gow,' in Spanish it means *'por favor no te vayas'.*" I stand up to get closer to her. "I don't know how you can understand that, but I hope you continue studying. You are still young. At eleven years old you can learn all the things you will need in life." She walks back to Mamá in the kitchen.

"Why don't you sit and I will make you some coffee, Aunt Lina?" I ask as I follow her. I want her to talk to me. "We have work to do. Go up into the tree to cut some mangos for Lina to take home," my curly-haired aunt interrupts me, and heads purposefully out the door to the cement sink, where we wash the clothes. Mamá and my aunts arrange themselves into a triangle, they talk and work at the same time.

"How is Teresa? Did she come back?" Mamá helps Aunt Lina set chairs in place and drops her own big black bag on the ground. Mamá settles herself comfortably to talk and to write down the things she needs from the Mercado Central. "I went yesterday to see if I could talk to her, but she was locked up in a room." Aunt Lina seems almost ashamed.

"What are you doing standing there, listening in on adult conversations? Go up to the tree and cut some mangos for your aunt." Mamá says to me, while curly-haired Tía Yita nods. I slip back into the house quickly to get a knife and a bowl in case I feel hungry for mangos up there. "Be careful going up. The tree can be slippery. It rained so hard last night," Aunt Lina says as I run to the ladder to go up on the terrace on top of the house. From there I can easily reach the mango tree, which although it grows from below, reaches up high over the little patio where my mother and aunts are seated. I climb quickly near the top of the mango tree. The branches are full of mangos. I clear off a small branch full of them, placing them in the bowl. From here, out of their sight, I see the three women talking freely, forgetfully unaware of my presence.

"How old was Teresa when the red old man came to her?" Mamá bites a ripe mango leaving red lipstick marks on it. "She was twelve," Aunt Lina puts an apron around her waist. "I am worried. Carmen is nine and once they turn twelve and the red old man comes, you cannot control them anymore." Tía Yita's pained voice does not slow her washing of the clothes. By this time I have shifted from the tree to the edge of the terrace where I dangle my legs.

"I took Teresa to church to see whether that would help her, but she just made fun of the Evangelics." Aunt Lina reaches down to pick up the hen my mother tied up earlier. She lays the hen on the table, slices off its head, and holds the hen still as its blood flows. My mother asks, "Did she bleed a lot?" "I didn't know about it until she was already pregnant." Aunt Lina pours water over the table to wash the blood off. "You were foolish to take her to the church. Now that evangelic man has locked her up in his house until he gets home from work." Mamá wipes the mango juice from her hands and the smudged lipstick from her mouth. "When the red old man scared me I didn't even realize it. I was working so hard on the tobacco farm," Tía Yita says as she washes my father's blue pants.

Mamá readies herself to go to the market. "I remember when Margarita was locked up in a house, too. Remember, Lina? That crazy man who nailed the door shut on Yita and nobody knew about it. Somebody came and told our Mamá that Margarita was missing and Mamá took a *tecomate* gourd and went to each corner of our house at noon calling Margarita's name into the gourd. She told us that the echo of the *tecomate* would reach Margarita wherever she was and make her desperate to do anything in order to escape any danger she was in." Tía Yita nods. "I remember I broke the door down and never saw that man again."

I lean back, lying flat on my back on the terrace, to look up at the open blue September sky. Teresa is only three years older than I, and now she is pregnant. I used to play hide-and-seek with her at her house. There were three houses on their barely developed dirt street, with a *cafetal* in front and a long tall wall to separate the skinny houses from the new rich *colonia*, called Jardines de Guadalupe. There was the tall *maquilisguat* tree with its pink flowers, the only tree we could climb on the whole narrow street.

My brothers and I used to play a game with Teresa called The Prisoner. We were the birds that fed the prisoner. We would lock her in her bedroom and then spend an hour passing fake and sometimes real food through the window. From the tree we connected a string to the window and let a plastic container slide to her with food and imaginary weapons inside to help her get out of jail. The food was sometimes mangos, leaves, flowers, or some bread that Teresa donated to the game. The weapons were stones, pieces of wood, sticks, and pieces of broken bottles we found in the trash of the rich people.

My sister Estela would climb with Teresa on top of the dining table and do go-go dancing. They would sing a song that always played on the radio in the afternoon, that goes "bule, bule," and another that goes "I guana hol iour han." My little brothers and I were the audience. They lifted their dresses above the knees to look like the girls in mini-skirts from the magazines my brother brought us from the rich *colonia*. Estela and Teresa's legs look like straws, they are so skinny.

I look down at Aunt Lina. She looks different, more still and calm than her sisters. On the weekends, she works as a midwife helping with the delivery of babies in the poor communities. She is so clean and organized as she washes up all the mess related to our chicken lunch.

Tía Yita says, "Teresa has been a fighter and a big-mouth since she was little, a complete devil. She talked back to me. How can this be happening to her?" She places white clothes in a bucket with water and bleach.

"Don't worry, Lina," says my mother as she puts a pot full of water on the wood burning stove. "She will get out of there." Mamá disappears back into the house to get ready to leave. I look hard at the other two women wondering where they hide the red old man.

"Well, I hope Carmen gets married and doesn't run around with men when the red old man comes. I will keep an eye on her so she doesn't have all the problems I did," Tía Yita says with a voice that sounds hurt, like the hens when my dad ties their legs so they cannot nest their eggs.

Mamá reemerges from the house looking very beautiful. She puckers her lips and says to her sisters, "Does it look all right?" Before they can answer, she turns and looks upward. "Where is Dalia? Is she still up in the tree? That little girl still wants to climb trees." "Well, she's eleven. You should be thinking about her," says Tía Yita. "Ah no, their father insists on keeping them at school and not letting them near boys until they have finished something." My mother's solidly sure voice always leaves my aunts silent. "Dalia! Dalia! Come down! I'm going to the market now."

I gather up the bowl of mangos and rush down the ladder. "Here I am." I face the three women with only my sad voice to protect me. "I don't want the red old man to scare me." The words come out loud like a Mexican ranchera that plays at five o'clock in the morning. The three women look at each other. Then, my two aunts return to their chores. Inside I feel as if my body shrank like an old ripe mango under the hot sun.

"You will be punished for listening in on adult conversations," says Mamá. I hug her. "Don't be foolish. No one will scare you." She returns my hug. I go out of the house, stand in the middle of the street to watch Mamá leaving. As she disappears from sight, the image of the red old man is right in front of me. He has two faces. One side of his face is like a man's, wrinkled with dark red lines in his teeth. He is laughing so hard that I want to pull his long bright hair and tie his mouth with it. But the other side of the face is a serious pale woman. She holds a red bag in her hand. When I try to touch her, she throws the bag in my face. I jump away from her, and land in the puddle of soft brown water, the exact place where I was playing before. I wonder why Mamá did not tell me the red old man has two faces.

The women coming back from their errands talk about what they are cooking for lunch. "I bought these big tomatoes to stuff them." One woman takes out a big red round tomato.

"I am going to prepare bean soup with pork bones," another woman says, looking at me in the puddle where I play, lost in my thoughts. "Look at this little girl still here. She just might become a little pig in the dirty water!" She points at me with her finger.

I stand in front of them quite seriously with my arms planted on my waist. "I know the red old man has two faces!" The women laugh hard, looking at me with pity. I come back inside my house and sit on the oval chair and think about the women's laughter, so similar to the laugh of the red old man.

...after...CAROLINA RIVERA ESCAMILLA

The Funeral

Papá says the cemetery is parched and infertile, like the woman we will bury. I know he speaks of his grandmother Isabel, who died two days ago. Until then I hadn't realized I had a living great-grandmother. I thought she must have died a long time ago.

Papá only mentions this woman whenever he remembers aloud for us, his children, how he met Mamá in 1951, and how he told her he had family. I think he only said this at that time, so he could be accepted as normal. He needed to say that he, too, had a family somewhere.

"Isabel is her name. She is a witch, a bad woman. She abandoned us, my sisters, and brothers and me on the streets when my mother died. She did not like my mother," he says hurtfully.

I ask, "Why are you here at her funeral?"

"She is my grandmother, after all. Where's the dead woman?" He asks and hands me a bouquet of royal blue verbena flowers to place somewhere in this house of the dead.

Papá's aunts advance to embrace my mother. The aunts turn their faces away from him. Estebana, the youngest, points with pursed lips and a turn-of-the-mouth to where the casket is. I place the flowers in the vase on the right side. Mamá signals with her eyes that I should greet these unknown aunts and behave with them as though I have known them all my life.

"Hi, how are you? I am sorry for the death of your..."

"Hi, how beautiful you are, child, so well-behaved." I fall silent to let the unknown aunt finish. I smile. No one has called me beautiful before. I think they like my smile, a smile that belies forced familiarity. Yet, still it pleases them.

I look at the silent hollow body inside the casket. The only living part of her is the moon-shaped green of a slice of lime placed between her lips. I wish I could have known this old lady when she was alive to ask her about my grandmother. My dad says my grandmother's name was Hortensia.

"Yes, I can tell you about her," says a voice. "What do you want to know?"

33

"Good afternoon. I am...I am... the daughter of Anton..."

"Demetrio."

"Yes, Papá has had many names in his life. There he is with the other men, looking for *chicha*." I say this wondering whether the dead body has come alive. I turn.

"Don't be afraid, little girl. I'm not Isabel. My name is Altamira. They call me the *chicha* seller." she says.

I must have said out loud the words 'I wish.' This old lady heard me, I guess, or she is a lady healer like those Papá says cure people.

"Your dad has every right to be angry with Isabel." Silvery long hair frames her wrinkled face.

"Who are you?"

" I was your great grandmother Isabel's best friend."

I feel calm before her face, like the face of my dog Capullo when he falls asleep at the side of the house. Her bronzed skin reminds me of the color of the muddy chocolate puddles the rain leaves after a storm. "I've heard about you. Papá talks about the woman who makes *chicha* from corn or sometimes pineapple, *panela de dulce*, and cane sugar wrapped in cornhusks. He says you ferment the mixture of the *panela* and the corn to make the alcoholic drink." I whisper this to her, because Papá says one can go to jail for making alcoholic beverages. "I thought he was telling us a fairy tale when he told us about you."

"Your dad is a good man. What do you wish to know about his mother?"

"Hortensia?" I ask softly, just to be sure whom she is talking about. "Did she make *chicha* like you?"

"Only once, before her baby died. I used to visit her in the *cantón* where your great-grandmother left her."

"What baby? Papá never talked about a dead baby. I know she died giving birth, but after my father was born."

"Perhaps he doesn't know about it."

"Tell me anything about her... tell me about her baby."

"I think she was older than you, almost fifteen," she says.

"I am fifteen," I say running my hand back through my hair. I straighten up and try to make my thin child's body look tall, like a soldier in front of his superior. She touches my right shoulder. I relax and return to my usual size. She knows I am lying. I am only twelve.

The *chicha* seller smiles and looks down at me as though I am the well to draw water from, but I need her to be the well from which to haul the story of my grandmother. "In 1917, Isabel had left her daughter Hortensia with Mascada and his wife when she was about two. Isabel just disappeared one day, never even saying goodbye to Hortensia. I used to go to check on Hortensia often. I was there the day they buried her son."

***

The bells rang with that solid and sure sound of mourning. On the steep road whose hilly shape sometimes caused the procession to dip out of sight as it climbed only to reappear moments later and climb again toward the church at the top, the sun shone tenuously. Children with thick black hair and slightly swollen bellies, their skin the color of baked clay, led the march toward the church. The youngest ones stayed back to hold their mothers' hands. Their clothing was worn, ill fitting and color-faded. Although some of the children moved playfully, their faces looked tired.

Little by little people from the *cantón* came closer. Four men, two young and two old, carried a litter on which rested a small wooden box painted white. Their faces expressed pride at being chosen to carry Alfonsito. They wouldn't see him anymore chasing the street dog that showed up outside the house at lunchtime and in the evening. They wouldn't see him smiling with his hand on a plastic bottle full of *café*, his other hand waving goodbye to them as they passed the house in the evenings. They wouldn't dream of becoming his father one day. They wouldn't be able to use him to flirt with Hortensia anymore.

She would scare them away by chopping at the trunk of the mango tree with her machete, leaving several wide gashes. The men would laugh and throw kisses at her. But now they lowered their eyes whenever she passed close to them.

Tacho made a wooden car for Alfonsito, for his second birthday. And a year later, he had made him a casket. He led as

35

one of the men at the head of the box.

"When will our children stop dying, God?" Tacho sighed deeply and kicked at the street dog that crossed his path.

Women with long thick black braided hair walked on both sides of the casket, some of them wearing black dresses, with white kerchiefs on their heads. The others were dressed in dark or pastel-colored dresses. Two of them recited *camándulas*, the five mysteries that adults pray, keeping count on the pinewood-beaded rosaries in their hands. Praying the rosary was not appropriate for a child's funeral, but they hoped it might stop the epidemic of children dying.

Decorating the white wooden box with white and baby blue crepe paper was appropriate for a three year-old child. Spilling over the box were purple, yellow, white carnations, orange wildflowers, and morning glories the children picked along the road toward the church.

Everyone finally came around to the front of the old whitewashed adobe church. The people settled themselves momentarily wherever they could, taking drinks from the water barrels with *morro* tree bowls. Padre Simón stood waiting inside the entrance of the church. On this occasion he went farther out than he would normally in order to meet the casket and to bless the body. Mascada, Alfonsito's godfather, had given him three healthy hens, so the priest would stay longer for Alfonsito's prayers. Tacho opened the box. Alfonsito lay inside, dressed in his white baptismal gown, his hands folded, interlaced fingers holding a white carnation, as though he were praying. His stomach was bulging. His feet and face looked like balloons full of water. Padre Simón blessed him.

"God bless you, child, in the name of the Father, the Son, the Holy Spirit, and of our Virgin who will embrace you with extended arms. Amen." The people drew closer to see him. The children surrounded the box and their mothers with questions.

"Where's he going, Mamá?"

"He's going with the *angelitos* like your sister Teresita."

"Why are his eyes open, Mamá?"

"His Mamá will close them."

The children always asked where the dead children went; each had lost a sister or a brother in the *cantón*. Five women encircled the casket, their eyes red and swollen from this morning's *parabienes*, chants for the dead children.

They whispered, "The child could have been saved if Hortensia would have followed the recipes."

"Ay *comadre*, don't say that. Hortensia gave everything she could to this boy. She is herself still a young girl and her destiny has been bent already by that evil spirit."

Mascada and el Choquito Santo, the two singers of the *parabienes*, made their way back to see Alfonsito's body.

"Poor boy. He was not lucky enough to be cured by our medicine."

"It seems that the herbs are losing their power to cure. This land has become cursed."

"Alfonsito's father must have damned this woman and the land. He has done harm to our medicine and our offspring."

"Well, I am tired. I don't think I will reach the cemetery. I don't like cemeteries since my two children died. Before, I used to visit the cemetery. It was such a peaceful place." El Choquito Santo hung his mandolin back on his shoulder and slowly walked away from the crowd.

Mascada said, "Ay. Me too. Cemeteries remind me of the death of my wife. I feel tired. I woke up this morning at three o'clock to rehearse the *parabienes*. Did I sing them right? Sometimes I wish I could forget the lyrics forever."

***

The five women, Margo, Felicia, Victoria, Zoila, and Pola woke up early, too, to sing the *parabienes* to Alfonsito. Hortensia stood crying behind the adobe house, her face against the wall. The wall provided no barrier to the chants and refused to console her.

Mascada, godfather to many of the children in the *cantón*, chewed tobacco leaves and spat on the floor. He looked at the small lifeless body, and began the parábienes chant.

"An angel is going to follow a new life, a new path. He's leaving us saying,

'Don't cry, mother, please.

Don't cry, because I am going to be with Jesus and the

37

angelitos in heaven."

The people cried more when Mascada and El Choquito sang, "Don't cry, mother."

Mascada wiped his eyes with the back of his left hand, spat again on the floor, and started another song.

"At four o'clock in the morning I have come to sing for an angel who goes to find a way to heaven to ask Jesus to bring his godfather and godmother to bless him for the long playful journey."

The godfather put his mandolin on the adobe floor, spat again and blessed the child.

"I commend you to God. I give you this blessing in the name of the Father, the Son and the Holy Spirit, and of our Most Blessed Mother who receives you with open hands. Amen."

The godfather finished his blessing as Hortensia entered the dark narrow room. She pushed past the women who held rosaries with *camándulas*, the carved beads of the San Pedro tree. She took the *Niño de Atocha* from the altar, spat on it, and threw it against the wall, behind which she had been crying during the singing. The five women and Mascada looked at the defiled *Niño de Atocha* on the floor. For a second, instead of the image of the Christ child, they saw a dead black dove collapsed on the parched floor.

Mascada restrained the impulse to spit his tobacco again. "*El Niño de Atocha* has been spat upon." He brought out from his back pocket a yellow handkerchief.

Zoila walked rapidly toward Hortensia and said, "Hortensia, foolish girl, are you crazy? Alfonsito will have a hard time now passing through the gates of heaven. Pick up the saint, and apologize to God for what you have done to him."

Hortensia kneeled to pick up *El Niño de Atocha*, hugged it against her chest, and wailed, "Forgive me, God, for having brought a child into this world without love. It's my fault this has happened. Why did I go alone to the *cafetales*? Why?"

The godfather squatted to hold Hortensia to his chest and said, "Dear child, it is not your fault that God has taken Alfonsito to him. Release yourself from this blame or else Alfonsito's soul will blow around this world where he does not belong anymore. Let him go for good."

38

Hortensia didn't stop crying. Mascada spat into his handkerchief, took the Saint from Hortensia, and said to it, "Too many deaths, too many miracles to be asked for, you must be tired of us." He spat into his handkerchief again and placed the saint next to Alfonsito's body to be buried with him.

***

In front of the church, a sixty year-old woman with long hair the color of ashes came toward Hortensia to embrace her. The sun was still bright in this high place, although shadows fell in the lower areas of the village. Hortensia pushed Victoria aside, looked up into the sky, tried to see beyond the clouds. Victoria was mid-wife at Hortensia's birth eighteen years ago and at Alfonsito's birth just three years ago.

"God has him in his hands now," said Victoria.

Hortensia's tears during the night's vigil moved one of the women to press a bowl against Hortensia's cheek to catch them. That bowl of tears was placed inside the coffin alongside Alfonsito's body, just above where Mascada placed the *Niño de Atocha*. It was sprinkled on the body at the time of burial as holy water so that his swollen belly and body might go back down to normal size.

Hortensia lowered her gaze, and then raised her eyes to look directly into Victoria's. She fell upon her, let loose a scream, deafening the entire village for a moment.

***

During full moons, fifteen year-old Hortensia escaped Mascada's adobe room by slowly easing herself out of her wooden bed. She stole into the night, carrying the light of the swollen moon in her arms. "I have your power, Moon. Do you step on your own shadow? Do the clouds create your shadow? Please let me step on my shadow tonight." She jumped backward and forward, side-to-side to catch her shadow. The barking dogs called her to bed again.

The National Guard sometimes surrounded the plantation, or her village. The women, who included her now, took care to give the soldiers food. Whenever the Guards noticed a group of peasants together, they kept their eyes on them. If they saw them drunk, or passed out on the side of the road on their way home, the soldiers nudged them with their rifles or rolled them over to see who they were. Sometimes the soldiers mumbled, "As long as these *Indios cabrones* behave themselves, who cares if they die from drinking?"

Hortensia stayed mute each time the guardsmen walked past her. One day she decided to smash tadpoles with a stone in the river close by her house.

"For each one of you I kill, I am killing one guardsman."

***

Hortensia's grandmother, Valentina, had five children, four sons and a daughter named Isabel. Valentina married well to a man who owned three *fincas*. In his mind, she captured him with her honey-colored eyes, robust hips, and the flow of her black hair. The oval shape of Valentina's face accentuated her delicately shaped lips with its timid smile. She was fourteen and he was thirty-three, and he took no other woman after her. Five years and five children later, someone who still loved Valentina since before her marriage stabbed her husband to death. Valentina then ran the farms. When the four sons all claimed the *fincas* in later years, Valentina divided the land among them. Three of the four died fighting among themselves. They spent almost all the money in the *burdeles* and *cantina* of the cantón.

Valentina hanged herself inside the house one night under a full moon. Isabel, then twelve, saw the lifeless shadow from her bedroom. The one remaining son sold the *fincas* and ran far away to the coastal villages to spend his money on whores. He disappeared forever on a boat to Colombia. A neighbor took in Isabel.

***

Isabel got pregnant at the age of thirteen by one of the helpers of the *chicha* seller.

"What have you done, Isabelita? You're sick. You look pale. Have you been hiding something from me?" The *chicha* seller asked in the cornfield.

"It happened when you went to the sugar cane fields and left me here alone. Narciso told me he wanted to show me butterflies in the cornfields. He says that on the backs of their wings are lucky numbers, and the next time he buys a lottery ticket, I will pick the numbers. He says the butterflies only reveal the lucky numbers to beautiful girls." Isabel's hands worked faster pulling the corn's leaves from the maize.

Twenty-five-year-old Narciso knew Isabel since she was born, and with hidden glances used to observe her body. Narciso did, in fact, believe that butterflies carry lucky numbers on the backs of their wings. As a child he used to spend hours chasing them, but never caught the mature orange and yellow ones, only trapped the baby ones. He believed the small ones brought love, because of the pleasure he felt cupping their tiny soft wings between his palms. On the day he stopped chasing them, he cried, and made a promise to himself by throwing a stone to the sun that one day he would find a woman to help him catch the lucky butterflies. Twelve years later, in the cornfields he discovered Isabel hurling a section of fish net, trying to catch butterflies.

"I got one. It has orange and black dots on its wings." She screams as she lifts the net and holds the butterfly gently between the palms of her hands. She opens a hole in her hands to show it to Narciso, her neighbor.

"Now, look at the back of the wings," he says.

"How? She will fly away." She pulls the butterfly protectively back. "Kill it with your palm." Isabel looks at him doubtfully, her heart-shaped face slightly grimacing. Her almond-shaped black eyes shift towards the sun, and she opens her hands, letting the butterfly fly away. Narciso goes silent, like walls at night. He pins her onto the field while she looks up to where the butterfly went, blinded by the bright peach light of the day.

***

One day while walking to the sugar cane fields, she saw a group of people pinching their noses with their fingers as they stood around the rainwater cistern.

"It stinks."
"What is that rotten smell?"
"The water's been poisoned."
They emptied the cistern, and found the body of a young man.
"Huy, God! It's Narciso."

***

Hortensia, like her grandmother, grew up in the midst of the *cafetales*, the coffee groves where she labored alongside her people from the *cantón* at the *finca* San Isidro. She worked hard from coffee tree to coffee tree with her basket belted to the front of her waist, cutting and picking the berries, tasting the sweet ripe ones from time to time. Sometimes she stepped on the ripe berries with her bare feet to feel the cold clammy juice on her skin. October's harvest was foretold by the light breezes, which lightly disheveled her hair as she returned from the constant chores of the *patrón*. Like a fallen leaf she floated from house to house announcing the coffee trees were waiting for their women.

Hortensia counted the months from January to October with her fifteen-year-old delicate fingers, until Mascada yelled at her to return to work. She raised her face to see the trees dancing with the wind. She climbed a *pepeto* tree to reach for a bird's nest, to see whether the wind had detached the baby bird from its home. As she descended from the tree, she felt hands at her waist, which pulled her down fast.

"Shh. Don't turn around." He has her by the hair. She cannot see his face. "Don't scream, or Mascada and you will lose the work." She hears the voice of the patrón. Hortensia lowers her head as he pulls her panties down.

***

In front of the church, Hortensia cried, "Victoria, why didn't you give my child good luck when he was born? The people say you have the hands of an angel to give life. Why is Alfonsito gone?"

The midwife replied, " God has taken him to be one of his angels. Alfonsito came into this life with the sign that he didn't belong in this world. His umbilical cord didn't show earthly signs."

Hortensia cried out, "God is not just with poor people, Victoria. Listen to me, God! Our children are dying in this *cantón* of parasites, of diarrhea, famine... where are you, God? Victoria, you're a witch. You killed my son. I trusted you to bring Alfonsito to live a full life in this damned *cantón*."

Victoria lowered her head. Alfonsito was the fifth child to die in the *cantón* within two months. Victoria always said the children were angels who came to earth by mistake. Alfonsito suffered with diarrhea for a week. Hortensia recalled that only his eyes were alive in the end, as his body could no longer respond to his mother's kisses, to his mother's touch. She remembered a healthy Alfonsito running to her, holding out his hands for her to warm with her kisses. Alfonsito and Hortensia would laugh and snuggle, and he would always fall asleep rubbing her ear. During those last days, no matter how much she tried, his hands remained cold.

She gave him all the boiled medicinal herbs the people of the *cantón* had recommended, and even the medicines Mascada had used on her when she was sick. One day it came to Hortensia's mind to ask around about a doctor, but this type of care was only for the rich people.

One woman in her thin house said, "Give him boiled *Sunza* seed." Another told her, "Cook the seed of mango with goat's rue." And yet others recommended boiled rice water or a pill for curdling mixed with two doses of bismuth powder. "Cook leaves of *epazote* with garlic." In other circumstances these remedies gave good results for other children, but not for Alfonsito.

The bell tolled two more times and the procession circled around the church toward the cemetery. The four men stopped to open the casket so Hortensia could close Alfonsito's eyes. More people joined in at the burial site. The sun went down, hid itself.

***

The next morning Hortensia awakened to undergo the pain of still living. She stooped to pick up Alfonsito's wooden car. A rusty nail stuck out and scratched her. She picked up Alfonsito's clothes, blew out the leftover candles, gathered the saints' holy cards, and the picture of the healthy white angels hanging from

43

clouds. Next came the big pictures of *El Corazón De Jesús*, the beautiful Virgin Mary, and the altar. Last was Alfonsito's bed.

Hortensia dragged everything outside, and built a pile in the shape of a volcano. She went back inside her house, and put on the red dress that made Alfonsito laugh. His smile would reflect back at him in the shiny satin and taffeta.

In the kitchen, yesterday's embers were still hot. She blew on the hot coals and lit a piece of paper. Hortensia set fire to the pile, starting with the saints. She sat down on a bench and watched the sparks and ashes as they rose up into the sky.

At three o'clock in the afternoon, holding two cotton bags, Hortensia stepped out of her tiny adobe house. The sun was starting to come out. She looked at the street dog lying in the yard, and the place where they had buried Alfonsito's umbilical cord. Staring at the *cafetales* in the distance, she smiled and closed her eyes as the wind danced in her hair. She spat at the air, and then disappeared. The only sound that echoed through the streets was, "¡Qué Dios vaya contigo, hija."

***

The chicha seller's old wrinkled hands hold mine tightly. I look at the corners of her eyes, at her wrinkles like ravines in the earth that channel tears to the ground. I guard the image of my grandmother in her red dress, my great-grandmother with butterflies in her hands.

***

"Dalia, Dalia, where are you, child?" My father calls. The funeral is ready to start.

"I was with the chicha seller. She knows your mother very well, and your grandmother, too, Papá." I sense my mother drawing up behind me.

"That old woman is walking history. She must be about ninety years old." My father grumbles, "The *chicha* has kept her alive all these years." I don't like his sarcastic tone and tell Mamá that I will walk with the *chicha* seller to the cemetery.

"You should come with us. I do not think she will come to the

44

cemetery," my mother says. I go to the *chicha* seller, who is in the kitchen lighting a candle from the wood fire. "Are you coming to the cemetery?" I take the candle from her.

"No, my daughter, I am too old to walk. Soon enough I will be carried to the cemetery, like my two sons, like Isabel and your grandmother." She takes the candle from me, walks to *El Corazón de Jesús* that hangs on the wall, and places the candle on an oak table below the picture.

"I want you to tell me more about my grandmother. Where did she go after Alfonsito's death?"

"What I can tell you is that she went to live in *cantón* Amate Marin, near Tres Ceibas, where she met your grandfather Benjamin. She had four children, one after the other. She died giving birth." She taps me on my head. "Ask Demetrio, your Papá. He knows how your Grandma and your Grandpa died." She puts something in my pant pocket, and tells me that it is for my father.

I go outside to meet the procession to the cemetery. Mamá is waiting for me. When I look back inside to thank the chicha seller, she is gone.

The cemetery is two miles away. Staying close to the casket, I talk to my great-grandmother in silence, asking her to find Hortensia in heaven, and to give Alfonsito a kiss. I imagine them as two girls like me, one chasing butterflies and the other chasing the wind. We arrive at the cemetery. The hole is already dug out. Four men place the casket all the way down. Like my aunts, I grab some of the freshly excavated dirt and throw it on the casket. They are crying. I cannot cry. Papá is the last one to grab some soil and sprinkle it on the casket. "Poor woman. We are burying a lot of secrets with her. She never loved my mother, me, nor any of my brothers and sisters. Who knows whom she loved?" my father mutters.

I want to answer that perhaps she did not know what love was, since no one loved her.

***

My parents stay in the car as they bid goodbye to the people from the *cantón*. I ask for the *chicha* seller, where she lives, but nobody seems to know.

45

Papá points, "---in the sugar cane fields cutting the cane to make *chicha*." I look hard at the cane fields as the afternoon sun's golden rays filter into the green cane leaves. The sight brings me a sweet-bitter memory of the women from my father's family. I feel sad and tired.

On the way home I imagine three women working hard together in the cane fields: mi *tatarabuela* Valentina moving her robust hips with the wind, and then her shadow hanging under a moonlit night; mi *bisabuela* Isabel holding an orange butterfly in her hands, and then hiding her morning sickness from the *chicha* seller by working, pulling the corn leaves faster from the maize; and mi *abuela* Hortensia in her red dress chasing the wind, and scaring the men away by chopping at the trunk of the mango tree with her machete.

Time of the Fattened Cows

1976's cicadas and their millions of babies take over all of nature with their unique sound emanating beautifully and possessively from bougainvillea trees dressed in yellow, pink, red flowering that let us know it's the Easter season. Usually during Easter we would hang out at the Lago Coatepeque, a routine every year since I started storing up memories. We used to go by bus, but now that Papá has more construction work, and Mamá manages all the money, they finally buy a used red Ford pickup from a friend who was visiting from Michigan. In that red Ford pickup we travel quickly and easily to the lake to take walks, to climb fruit trees, and to swim. We build campfires and sleep lakeside, listening to the calls of wolves, coyotes, owls, and other birds.

This Easter of 1976 is different, though, in that our parents decide to depart with us for Mexico. This idea strikes us as amazing, as a fantastic journey. The possibility of such a departure day to a magical place only becomes real for us children the day Papá's construction workers begin building a skeleton of wood and start covering it with canvas in the bed of the pickup. Papá does not want it made out of wood but of metal pipe to make it more windproof. However, it is too late for finding such material, as the supposed scheduled time for departure is running close.

Papá's adventurous expeditions seem always to require spontaneity. With only a week's planning, the whole family, including the dogs, and one of Papá's friends, Chele Pavián, a reliable construction worker, who happens to be walking along the road, will drive off to México. We are fourteen people, with nine passports, eleven of us children. One passport will supposedly cover four of us children. On short excursions, Mamá counts us every time we jump into the red Ford pickup. Papá designs and pays his construction workers to put a wood railing all around the interior of the bed of the truck for us to hold onto for our protection and stability, if we want to move

47

around in transit. The railing is independent of the eventual canvas covering that forms a roof. "We are gypsies!" Papá announces, as we jump inside the back of the pickup. We have never seen gypsies, so Papá explains that they are people who wander around the world without permission, permits or respect for any borders. "Passports are just a bureaucratic way for governments to make money and to control lands and people," he declares and then lets out a shrill whistle to call over the driver. The driver is the middle son from the Witch family, *Los Brujos*, in a time when we're still at peace with them. We imagine all the people from the *colonia* coming out as we pass their houses to wish us luck on any journey as we set out on the Main Street, *la Calle Principal*. This year, the big journey to Mexico is in the middle of March, almost the middle of Easter vacation. Even though Easter vacation is only for a week, we find out we can bury our boring beige school uniforms and white socks under our beds for two weeks.

The last dry winds and hot burning rays of March dance on our heads and bodies, as we wait early morning outside in line for the passports at some kind of government building. It's the first time we've ever seen anything like this big building. My big and little brothers, my sisters and I look like we are dressed with hair combed for a birthday party. We are all wearing seriously sleepy expressions. Mamá carries our baby brother, eleven-months-old in her arms, while Papá presses forward in line in front of us. Estela and I walk around tending to little brothers and sister, as they make small noises, like cooing pigeons. As always in public, nothing escapes from our mouths as loud or as alarming as the noisiness we make at home. Angel and Reinaldo, my two older brothers, wear their wavy and curly hair long. Angel's necklace and Reinaldo's metal peace symbol dangling from a leather string loop around his neck over his tight shirt represent very much the latest in style. These brothers check on all of us from a distance, having expelled themselves from the line. We guess it not to be "cool" to be seen standing with us in the line with Mamá and Papá. Besides, my little brothers and sister are growing tired and hungry, and are complaining quietly about the morning coolness. Estela and I laugh because they are confused as to why we are even experiencing this morning's cool breeze. In fact, even though the morning is nice and fresh, it has already been three hours since we have come here to wait in line, and the March sun is warming up to bake our impatient skin. Edwin scratches his head complaining that he has fleas. We laugh covering our mouths. He is saying this because he says he has just seen a street dog lying alongside the street. Sure enough there is a street dog that has lain down several meters away. "You don't have fleas." I walk over and kick the dog to get it to go away.

The line moves slowly ahead and finally we are inside the building. It's our turn for passport pictures. A man asks Mamá to group all the very little ones together. Mamá stands Mauricio, Edwin, and Noe side-by-side, while the man brings a chair to seat baby Abraham next to them for the picture. One passport and one photo will be enough for all the littler ones. Next are individual pictures of Janet, Javier, Antonio, Estela, me and of my hippie brothers, who fix their hair for a professional picture. Polaroid photos are distributed to Mamá and Papá. "Easy as things should be," Papá says and leads us to another line. When the people in charge see how many children we are, they move fast for fear of so many littler kids, already giving signs that they might start crying at any moment. Within what seems like only minutes, Mamá's bag carries our eight new passports.

On the way back to the house, we notice purple morning glories that have recently appropriated our neighbors' humble fences, along the dirt borders of Main Street. The whole family of eleven siblings beams greetings to the neighbors. March's sun reveals its force against the corrugated metal walls and roofs of our *colonia*. People walk slowly. Mamá's three-and-a-half-months of pregnancy is starting to show. Some aunt says that Papá should probably wait for Mamá not to be pregnant, but we are all so used to seeing her pregnant, Papá probably dismisses her pregnancy as unimportant, and we children do not want to delay the adventure either.

A day before the trip to Mexico, my sister and I go with Mamá to buy clothes for the trip. We go to Kismet, the place where my two older brothers buy their clothes. The store is always filled with the latest clothes, and the disco music is loud. Like my mother, I choose baby-blue bell-bottom polyester pants, but with small black polka dots on it, and a matching kite blouse. My sister gets the same outfit in yellow, as does my little sister in pink. Then we see the shoes. "Mamá, look at these shoes... they are made of wood!" So she buys three pairs of platform shoes, like hers.

On the morning we are supposed to leave for Mexico, the four of us females look like models out of a clothing catalogue, even Mamá with her slightly swollen belly. Mamá looks so tall with her baby-blue polyester bell-bottom pants suit and her platform shoes. She puts on bright carmine red lipstick and pink powder for her cheeks. When she smiles, her teeth look like they are inside a red rose. She looks happy. My father wears his navy blue suit and his blue tie with soft gray stripes on it. My little brothers are all dressed in bell-bottom polyester pants, too. My two older brothers are wearing bell-bottom blue jeans, each with a symbol of peace and love around their necks. "Yanet, put this on." Mamá hands my little sister a polyester gray-blue color jumpsuit with red ducklings to put over her pink polka dots. The atmosphere is of great pride, like the energy of a national festivity. We seem like summer ants running from one place to another. Even Nata, our store credit lady, and the neighbors carry some of our excitement in their eyes and hands. We feel like dancing, exhibiting similar emotions among us, the travelers who are leaving soon. Just as we are ready to leave, we line up for a Polaroid picture---ten pictures actually. The older brothers and sisters help the smaller ones to fall into place in the pickup, and each one of us is supposed to be aware of his or her own bags with clothes. When everything is ready, and we are inside the pick up, we drive to Antiguo Cuscatlán to finish installing and adjusting the canvas and to fill the orange and blue plastic containers with extra fuel, containers that are with us in the back of the pickup. The fuel containers are tightly wrapped in a rug and rope. "Do not let any fire around this or you will explode and the adventure will be over." Papá lifts his hand looking up the sky. "It is our father's sage advice," he says.

In those photos, my little brothers hang from my mother's pants, the smallest one crying---the others with sleepy faces. Papá distributes the pictures to the neighbors and to Tía Yita. "Keep it as a souvenir of the first big trip taken by one of the families of this *Colonia Rubio*. Next time it will be you." My father behaves as though he is the first astronaut to the moon. He takes a handful of *colones* from his pocket and throws them to the kids who come to say goodbye to my little brothers. My sister, Estela, and I say goodbye to Mila, our friend, and we tell her, "We are going to bring you a picture of El Zorro, and we will tell him that you want to meet him." Mila smiles and says, "Bring me one of the Beatles, too." "Yes!" says my sister. I jump on the truck and ask my older brother, "The Beatles--- do they live in Mexico?" "No, they are from England." I jump down from the truck to tell Mila, "The Beatles are from England, but maybe my father will want to go all the way there. We will take a picture of The Beatles, and tell them that you like their music and their hair, but if we don't go to England, we'll bring you the picture of El Zorro only." My two older brothers blow kisses and wave goodbye to their girlfriends, the daughters of the Witches, and the pickup takes off for Mexico.

When I yell, "Papá, the canvas has flown off the back of the truck," I inhale a face full of dust, that sticks in my throat, but who cares---we're going to Mexico. Papá brings the heavy grayish-green canvas as a canopy to tie over the back of the pickup, to shelter us from the harshness of wind at high speeds and from any rains, as the covered truck also has to serve as our camp-out bedroom. I stick my head out one more time to say bye to everyone, including the street dogs that are chasing us and barking, until they get tired, and take their barking back to the *colonia.*

Our driver, El Junior Brujo Tavares, whose real first name is Roger, comes from the family up the street whose daughters date my older brothers. We have a strange relationship with this family. They seem more numerous than us: daughters, sons, cousins, nephews, nieces, and more people whose family relationships we cannot figure out. The family has big trucks that carry cows, pigs, and even horses. People resent them, as they take over, crowd, and often block the two main streets that make up the *colonia*. The streets are only dirt roads, and their heavy trucks, especially in the rain, have broken down both streets. The heavy rains make a constant mess everywhere, but especially where we are living, a hundred meters down the street from the *mesón* they inhabit. Unfortunately, my older brother, Reinaldo is totally in love with one of these *brujos'* daughters, and she is madly in love with my brother, too. "How do we separate them?" Papá asks. "There is nothing we can do to separate them. forcing them apart would only make things worse." Mamá says.

Mamá and Papá are not happy about this relationship. Since we do not know any other experienced drivers, Junior Brujo Tavares, who is always available to be a driver for Mamá, becomes our hired driver to take us to Mexico. Mamá thinks he is at heart a good young man. Unfortunately for him, Mamá La Bruja Grande, whose mouth is sharp like a Gillette razor blade, is corrupting him. Junior Brujo, under my Mamá's direction and care, is like a good Mormon. Besides Angel and Reinaldo get along with him, and consider him a good friend.

The construction worker Chele Pavián , whose preference is really to sell coloring books and colored pencils, got this name from Papá, because Papá says he is like the white monkey from the zoo, who is considered by the public as both fearful and charismatic. Chele Pavián has even accepted that he looks like this animal. As we encounter him on the streets while leaving for Mexico, Papá asks him to get in the pickup, if he wants to go with us to Mexico. My sisters, brothers and I are not happy that he is joining us, as we are already cooped up in the small space of the pickup bed. Now this tall man, whose feet stink, is taking up a lot of space. We like him sometimes because he brings us notebooks, coloring books, and colored pencils.

At about five-thirty p.m. we are finally heading for Mexico. Darkness soon falls. We like to lift our heads out through open seams in the flapping canvas to see how dark it's all around outside. The sky is brilliant with stars above. In less than three hours we arrive at the immigration station between Guatemala and El Salvador. Only Angel and Reinaldo get down out of the pickup to assist our parents. We, who stay awake, see the yellow flicker of lights outside through the opening. On the way to the first border crossing, we are eating candies and other goodies. El Chele Pavián is watching us and throwing out nervous laughter from time to time, perhaps because we are getting close to the border of Guatemala with El Salvador, and he is not carrying a passport. During what seems an endless stop at the immigration checkpoint in Guatemala, even though it's still early in the night, we stay inside the pick up. Mamá and Papá get out to bring the passports to authorities, while el Chele Pavián slips from the back of the pickup to walk the periphery of the border station. He is trying to hide from the immigration officers. After everything is finally checked out and approved, we start to enter Guatemala, and then Chele Pavián flags down our pickup about a half-a-kilometer into Guatemala. He jumps back into the pickup. It's raining lightly, which we think is fantastic for us, as the unbearably feet-stinking stifling heat inside under that canvas lifts a little. After a couple of stops to relieve ourselves at the side of the road, and after traveling most of the night, we arrive at the border between Mexico and Guatemala and again Chele Pavián has to avoid immigration agents. The immigration officials are easy-going, as they check all our passports, and we leave. Chele Pavián uses the same plan to go around the border before dawn, but does not realize until later that he has to deal with a second immigration checkpoint inside Mexican territory in broad daylight. He no longer has an escape plan. Without knowing what to do, poor Chele Pavian, is panicked and follows Papá's and Mamá's instructions to crawl under Mamá's long maxi-skirt. Since Papá announces to the border agents that Mamá is pregnant and cannot easily get in and out of the pickup, the agent does not even care about seeing her. Once past this final checkpoint, we come to a village center, where we look for a place to park, to get out of the pickup to stretch and move about. Only then does el Chele Pavián come out entirely from under Mamá's skirt.

There are a lot of people in this village who are buying things at an outdoor market. Mamá, Papá, Angel, and Reinaldo go out to exchange our *colones* for *pesos* at the bank. We are getting frustrated due to the hot sun cooking us in the back of the truck like chickens in a pot. We are whining, and fights are starting among us. We two older sisters get out of the pickup, and roll the canvas back a little. Roger and Chele Pavian have no idea what to do with us, as they do not want to be responsible for us children. They slowly walk away to a park that is nearby. We can see Mamá checking on us from a distance. We all begin to calm down when everyone returns with ice cream for each one of us, bought from an old man passing by with his cart. Although happy to be eating ice cream, we make ourselves a sticky mess. Mamá looks like she is glowing like a ripe, red pomegranate. From carrying our youngest baby, she is tired, in apparent anguish, and pregnant.

We continue to Tapachula, where we eat tacos, a new food for all of us. We like the park in Tapachula, surrounded by buildings. We see people sitting on benches, under the many trees. We sit to finish our tacos under what looks like a tamarind tree. We then get back in the pickup to drive down to a house where we see monkeys swinging, parrots singing, and children watching us. We park, and Mamá, followed by Papá, ask the adults on the property whether we might settle in for the night at the edge of their building, which has an open, partially paved, but dusty area like a soccer field where children play. We eat dinner and sleep in the pickup. I wonder whether we're almost like gypsies now.

The next day we awake, when it's already bright outside, but still very early. We listen to the soothing sound of a creek. The sweet people of the house have made us a delicious breakfast with the same kind of skinny tortillas used to make the tacos we ate the day before. Mexican tortillas are different from ours that are thicker and smaller circles. With the tortillas we devour something called *huevos rancheros* over fried beans with spicy hot salsa, accompanied by cups of *café con canela*. Mamá thanks these generous people for their hospitality. We know from the style and taste of the food that we are some distance away from El Salvador. After brief contact with the creek to splash our faces, we continue our trip toward Mexico City. That is our destination. For us kids, we would have been happy to stay in Tapachula.

After three more hours of driving, we stop around one o'clock to shake out our legs in an arid place, a desert. Not far from us, a short distance into the hills next to the highway, we stop and step out of the pickup to see what look like giant animals. They are rocks and boulders, though. We imagine them as turtles, dinosaurs, pigs and other objects shaped from rocks. It's more fun than looking for shapes in the clouds, because these shapes are here on earth, and might move, if we imagine hard enough. Angel sits atop what looks like a golden *torta* or Mexican *pan dulce,* and Reinaldo takes his picture. We children are not allowed to go up on these rocks. Only Roger El Junior Brujo, Chele Pavián, and my older brothers go out and over into the giant rocks. We just wave to them. They look like figurines, not like real people, on the big rocks. Finally, they descend and get back into the pickup.

We know we are about to arrive in Arriaga, when Papá starts yelling, "Look, look at that immense river." He asks to stop the pickup. Roger makes a sudden stop on the edge of the road and is not very well parked. Papá gets out, runs around to the back of the pickup, and opens the tailgate. He tells us to get out and go take a swim in the river. He sounds excited, and we think for a second he is electrified, as though an electric current from just seeing the river has charged him through. Now he is not wearing his navy blue suit and his blue tie anymore. None of us looks nicely dressed anymore on the trip. We older ones jump out of the pick up, and run downward fast toward the river with an unfolding plan to swim with our clothes on. I walk instead of running. Even from fifty meters, the clear water of the river looks like a mirror. Neither Papá nor we bigger children think about Mamá and our driver in the front of the truck and our little brothers still sleeping in back at the time Papá asked to stop.

Roger and Mamá wake up my littler brothers. Mamá asks Roger Junior Brujo to park the pickup better, and asks my littlest brothers to sit down, to hold onto the rail, and not to move until the truck is correctly parked. I hear all this as I walk down toward the river. I feel as electrified as Papá as I see the immense shimmering river.

Papá takes off his shoes, shirt, and pants and is already in the deep part of the river. My older brothers are partially undressed and swimming toward him. We girls are just dipping our feet in the water, when we hear a sudden loud bang and screams. We run up to the road, and see Mamá crying and my little brothers screaming. Javier is bleeding from the mouth. Papá, Angel, Reinaldo, and El Chele Pavián are almost already there, as they put on their clothes, run and climb at the same time. We see that the pickup has been hit and pushed farther up the road. Javier hit his mouth on the back of the truck cabin; Noe hurt his elbow. Mamá and the Roger El Junior Brujo are still seated in the cabin, but are moving. Mamá's head is hurt. She hit it on the dashboard; baby Abraham is ok, still calm and happy in her arms. Two women step forward and identify themselves as daughters of a government official, as they gesture toward their vehicle. Javier is carrying Noe toward the tailgate. Papá helps Mamá to get out of the car, and Angel and Reinaldo, help my brothers get down very carefully. Roger pushes hard to be able to open the driver-side door. The pickup is hit hard, knocked several feet within a few inches of the edge of the incline heading steeply down toward the river. The car has hit the truck hard, side-swiping the whole length of the driver's side. The two women who hit us were responsible for the accident, but make us swear we are the guilty ones. "After all," one of them says, "you are not Mexicans, and we are the daughters of the governor of Chiapas." Their small car's passenger-side is totally smashed up, but they are not hurt. Papá is still very electrified, and even offers the two women money. They decline and left us there right away. For us, there is no choice. We have to locate a mechanic to repair our vehicle. We all surround Mamá, while Papá, Chele Pavián, Angel and Reinaldo flag down a car to go look for help. Roger Junior Brujo stays with us. He looks so pale and lost, needlessly taking blame, as if he has shattered our illusions of him as a good driver. Mamá, who is paler than usual, passes the baby to Estela, and offers him a glass of water, and says, "This is not your fault. Thank God we are alive."

Regardless of the heat, we do not go back down to the river. We stay with Mamá, seated in a bit of shade on the side of the road. We start counting the cars going by, until finally we see a big tow truck coming from the direction Papá and my brothers have taken to get help. We are directed to jump into another pickup that stops for us behind the tow truck. The men do what is necessary to tow our pickup. We drive toward the mechanic's garage. In silence we look at one another. We see how hungry and tired we are in our bodies and faces. We look ahead at our red pickup and are sure the towed red pickup we are following will be crying soon, too, as it realizes that neither it nor we are going to see Mexico City.

Baby Abraham awakens after a nap on Mamá's lap. We see him as we look into the cabin from the back window. His smile invites us to answer him with a smile, too. After an hour, we arrive at the mechanic's garage, which is not at all close to a city or a village. The tow truck driver drops off the red Ford pickup under a tamarind tree that is full of leaves and dripping with fruit pods. Meanwhile, the driver of the second pickup drops us next to our wrecked vehicle. Four of us older ones help the little brothers and sister to get out of the pickup. The second driver waves to the owner-tow-truck-driver-mechanic of the place, and then drives away. The tamarind tree creates a lot of shade, and the sun is not as strong in the late afternoon as it was when we experienced the accident. The mechanic is the owner of the shop and lives at this place, which is only a little workshop with a little store attached to it, with a large patio in front of it. Papá arranges with the mechanic for us to stay overnight sleeping in our damaged pickup. We still have food we have purchased for the trip and can buy some things inside the mechanic's store. We like the place because it has the big patio and we can keep playing until late. We lie on the patio counting the thousands of stars, which late at night are very visible. We gather and eat some of the ripe tamarind that no one else has thought to pick up. We sleep under this protecting tree. Mamá cooks over a small fireplace campfire Papá creates from bricks he has the boys carry from behind the mechanic's garage. After three days of battling mosquitoes and sleeping under an open sky, the pickup is finally fixed. We hear Mamá quietly telling Angel and Reinaldo, "Go into the city of Arriaga to buy some souvenirs. We will be returning to El Salvador tomorrow, even though your Papá wants to continue." Angel asks Mamá if he can take El Chele Pavián and Roger El Junior Brujo. At first she says softly, "Yes," but then immediately changes her mind, saying, "No, do not ask them to go. Just go with Reinaldo. They may find a way to follow you anyway, but do not tell them you are buying any souvenirs, because they are going to tell your Dad. No matter what, I have decided to return home tomorrow and not to continue this trip. Just pick up key chains and other little things for your sisters and little brothers." She hands him a bunch of pesos. "This should be enough to buy everything."

Angel, Reinaldo, Roger El Junior Brujo, and Chele Pavián return late night. We hear murmuring voices mixed with the sounds of mosquitoes. We dream a river passing through. In the morning Mamá gives my sisters and me pink, yellow, red, blue, gold, and silver thin bracelets that in the sunlight shine brighter than the stars of the Arriaga sky. For my little brothers Mamá distributes hats, little cars made of aluminum, and key chains as gifts for our friends at school.

Going through customs on our return to El Salvador is easy. When we are entering El Salvador, Papá asks Roger to stop the car. Mamá reminds Roger to park well off the road. There Papá orders us to stand beside the pickup. He removes the entire canvas from the wood skeleton so we can feel free in the open air. Once we are back in the pickup, Mamá gets out of the truck cabin and asks us, "Would you like to go to el Lago de Coatepeque?" We all scream yes like in a chorus of parrots.

We arrive home at midnight. We never tell the neighbors what happened to us. Mila never asks for the Zorro photo, as though she understands our silence about the trip. We give her three thin red, blue, and gold bracelets. She likes them. Not even Roger El Junior Brujo gives away this secret. We cherish the fifty something shiny multi-colored bracelets (Mamá and Papá find them everywhere in the house for weeks.) and the starry nights from our trip to Arriaga, Mexico.

The Baptized

The light of the moon allows me to see his face and hands. The brown burgundy leaves of this season match his skin's texture and color. He is darker than me because he has spent years under the sun building mansions, schools, and gas stations. Papá speaks to us in groups whenever he wants to talk about how he learned to build mansions. Otherwise, he only tends to speak to us individually by giving us orders to do some chore or to fetch something for him. When we were younger, he talked to us in groups, as though, by doing that he was taking on the authority or playing the role of a father. These days, however, and on this evening under the moon of September, I am older, eighteen years old as we share this space. He and I are like this unfinished three-storey construction we share tonight. We love the incompleteness of the space we share, even as we choose to sit separately on this grand terrace.

Last week when we got on the bus going to downtown San Salvador, my sister and I were surprised to see him in the bus, and said, "Papá!" He stood up, gave us his seat, and got off at the next stop. "Take care, and do not come home too late!" We know he is always looking for work. Later when we arrived home, we told Mamá, "We saw Papá on the bus." She answered, "He did not tell me he saw you girls."

"Who taught you how to build houses?" I shift my legs into a lotus position. "The engineer, Villaseñor Barahona. He was the first to teach me seriously about construction and blue prints. But before him in Sonsonate I learned from Miguel Rivera whose family name I took because he had become for me like a father, when he took me into his family." I had heard my father's story since I was about seven years old. Simply asking anything about his past seems to restore his strength and pride, at least momentarily. The present leaves him with empty pockets, eleven children to feed, an unfinished mansion, a son in Mexico trying to get far enough north to cross the border into the US. Papá has a wife who prays constantly for God to bring life back to this home. All the engineers my father ever worked for are leaving or

60

have left the country. Papá doesn't know whether he will ever find a job again. Mamá blames him for his drinking. Papá insists he lost the job because he protested for his rights and the workers' union did not support him.

"Why didn't you take *Tatita* Juan Reyna's last name? After all, he was the one who first picked you up as a boy on the streets and took you to his cave, and the only grandfather we used to know from your adopted family. Why did you take the last name Rivera?" "Juan Reyna was already very old when he took me to his home. The person who really raised me was his daughter Ramona, who married Miguel Rivera. I love Tatita Juan Reyna. He taught me how to fish in the deep green waters of El Lago de Coatepeque. His skills came in handy, as they helped me survive by eating fish. However, it was Miguel Rivera who showed me the world. It was he who showed me how to start a life of my own." He laughs, and then goes silent. "How did Miguel Rivera show you the world? Is he still alive? Did he baptize you? You always told us you had different names when you were young?" For a moment I feel like an eight-year-old, asking about his life as though it is homework for school. Although I know his story, I want him to tell me one more time ... I enjoy hearing it.

In the town of Los Naranjos in 1946 on a bus going to El Puerto de Acajutla, Demetrio Linares Molina is fifteen years old. "*Señores y señoras*, my name is Centavito, like the pennies you spend on candies for your children. I have rolled and spun around in circles like *un centavo* most of my life, until one day I happened to step on the shoes of this man here with the guitar. After I tripped over his feet, he picked me up and has been taking me around the world trying to make of me an honest citizen." "Thank you Centavito. Thank you. Today I will sing *El Cafetalito*, and Centavito will do a harmonizing second voice." Since Miguel Rivera and Centavito don't have the money to pay their bus fare to El Puerto de Acajutla, they make arrangements with the bus driver to let them sing songs on the bus to keep everyone entertained. "Get in, the people need some music to forget the heat of the day." The bus driver goes to close the front doors behind Miguel and Centavito after quick negotiations. "Be careful, boy, with your feet. You should make some shoes out of old tires for yourself." The driver watches Centavito leap barefoot onto the metal steps inside the bus doors. Miguel starts strumming guitar and singing *El Cafetalito*. Centavito pulls out a black comb and hums through it as a harmonica to help fill in Miguel's melody. Some people listen quietly. Some start laughing. A baby wakes up when the song starts. When Miguel finishes, Centavito removes the thin tobacco paper from the harmonica comb, and puts both comb and paper inside his pocket. "Thank you." People applaud and ask for another song. Centavito steps forward to ask for tips, but Miguel stops him. "Thank you. Before we take your tips, I want to baptize Centavito in front of all of you here." Centavito stands erect with his skinny arms crossed, as though he's in front of a church, even though he does not have a clue as to what Miguel is talking about. Miguel extends his right hand forward like a priest and blesses Centavito with the sign of the cross. "Your name will now be Antonio Rivera. Hence forth, you have a father, a brother, a family." Miguel finishes the baptism by playing another song, *Maria Bonita*, and Centavito-turned-Antonio plays his harmonica. Before they get off the bus at El Puerto de Acajutla, people drop spare coins into the hands of Miguel and Antonio Rivera. An old man gives Antonio a freshly cut coconut. "Drink some and sprinkle the rest on your head to finish your baptism." "Thank you." Antonio takes the coconut and helps the man down the steps of the bus.

...after...CAROLINA RIVERA ESCAMILLA

The King of Farts

The bus driver invites Miguel and Centavito-now-Antonio to eat dinner at a place around the corner from the bus terminal. "Ey, boys I know someone here who can give you a job." "Yes sir, we don't have work. We just sing on the street and now on the buses. We can learn to do any job." "Well, the boy you just baptized is really young, but you are older. How old are you?" "I am eighteen," Miguel says, "but for a fifteen-year-old, Centavito-now-Antonio has worked a lot and is a hard worker." Miguel chews his tortilla and pats Centavito-now-Antonio's shoulder. Centavito-now-Antonio stands, rubs his hands together and does push-ups on the old red tile floor. "Get up boy, I know you're strong," says the bus driver. "Well, the job is working on a boat, fishing, cleaning the fish, and it pays two colones a day, plus you can eat and sleep for free there and play your music too." "We'll take it," Centavito-now-Antonio says as he swallows his last bite. Miguel rolls up his white washed-out shirtsleeves and sighs, "When can we start?" The bus driver pulls out his wallet and gives one colon to the tanned one-armed waiter who serves them.

The boat belongs to a Colombian businessman. Centavito-now-Antonio feels right at home with the fishnets. Miguel is not sure about fishing, since his jobs were always related to the coffee harvest or to playing his guitar in bars. The boss gives the pair of men a fishing boat. They have to start at four o'clock in the morning and return by eight the same morning with several sea trout. "Centavito-now-Antonio, your feet are peeling. I think it's from the salt." "It's fine, they don't hurt. We're going to make money and buy new shoes for you and me. Look! Yours are torn in front." Centavito-now- Antonio touches Miguel's toes that are sticking out of a shoe. "We're not going to make money with this job. It's hard to get as many fish as the Colombian wants. We have to find another way to cultivate coins." Miguel nods to the sunrise. "Better yet, why don't we go to Colombia? Let's go now with this fishing boat.

Besides we're not throwing the net properly in the right position. We should be doing that instead of talking." Centavito-now-Antonio stands and poises himself in the correct position to throw the net. "You're the fisherman, Centavito-now-Antonio. Study the water and find those fish. I have a plan for tonight. We're going to gamble with the men from the other boats." Miguel leans over the edge of the boat and passes his flat hand lightly over the cool blue water. "Ey, I think I caught a thousand fish. Look! Miguel. Today we will have money to play." Centavito-now-Antonio pulls up the net with its dozens of moving fishtails.

That night they find the other fishermen where they usually are, on the deck of one of the bigger fishing boats playing craps. One man is called the king of craps and also the king of farts. No one has proven capable of dethroning the "King of Craps and Farts." "One, two, three, four, five, six, seven, eight, nine, ten, do you want more? Do you want me to save them in a bottle so that you can count them better?" says the king as he stretches his ribs on one side and then the other. He scrunches down, contorts his face, and forces an eleventh fart. All the men laugh. He has already beaten five men, and one of them can fart ten farts in a minute. The winner gets two colones, which is a day's pay. "He's full of farts. I think his mother gave birth to a fart, and must have given him cabbage to eat every day at every meal." "And his luck at craps? Where does that come from?" "From his father, of course. The son of a bitch is a son of a devil. No one can fart as much as he does and not die."

"But God farts too," interjects Centavito-now-Antonio. "He can be a son of a god, too, and that's why he doesn't die," "Ey boy, who are you? Ha! You guys are new." The King of Farts stares at Miguel and Centavito-now-Antonio. "You want to compete with me in farting?" "No, your farts are fat, and who knows where your farts come from, the devil or God?" "You're too young, boy. Only big, strong asses can compete with me. Who's ready?" The hero of farts positions himself on all fours to start another competition.
"I'll play craps against you." Centavito-now-Antonio says, "Hm, craps time, eh?" The hero gets up and straightens his pants. "How much money do you have?"

65

"We have ten *colones*, my brother and me." Centavito-now-Antonio points at Miguel who's been quietly studying the crowd.

Centavito-now-Antonio learned how to manufacture dice when he lived with Juan Reyna in the cave. He created a pair this afternoon specifically to win against the King of Farts and Craps. His dice have six black spots on the four sides. Centavito-now-Antonio knows how to hide the good dice and throw his trick dice in order to win. The men watch and laugh as Centavito-now-Antonio wins. The King is sweating and breathing faster than normal.

"You're a son of a bitch. What do you have there in your fingers? Open your hand." "Nothing in my hands." Centavito-now-Antonio passed the bad dice to Miguel, who is right next to him.

"Last one. Put all the money, lay it all on the ground," the King of Farts shouts wiping his sweaty forehead. "Yes, sir." Centavito-now-Antonio shakes the dice in his hands. The King of Farts throws his dice first. Centavito-now-Antonio takes the good dice, switches them one last time in his fingers and throws the bad ones. All sides have six black holes. He wins again, this time for two hundred colones. The King shouts and lifts the rock from the deck under which he has been pooling his money all evening. There's no money left. He places his right hand flat and smashes the rock on his own fingers.

Miguel and Centavito-now-Antonio catch a bus right away to the mountains bordering La Libertad, in the next province. The next day in Tepecoyo, Miguel buys Centavito-now-Antonio a pomegranate-colored pair of shoes that are just about as big as boots. They separate for some days, Miguel staying in town to sing in bars, and Centavito-now-Antonio going off to work in the *fincas* or coffee plantations.

...after...CAROLINA RIVERA ESCAMILLA

Macario

Papá begins his stories as though he's living them again, as though it is still the first time, as though the things he tells us, his children, are still happening. He does not realize that his stories include a lot of cursing and even sex. His monologues allow him to relive his brave survival in the time before he had a family.

"Antonio, don't forget you have this house because of me keeping you straight. Otherwise, you could have ended up like Macario," Mamá tells Papá. We are all outside the house, in the space between the wooden house and what we hope one day will be the big new house. Mamá is preparing to cook dinner.

"Woman, I am talking about my life before I met you." Papá stands in front of Mamá, protecting himself with a defensive look. He then sighs, and I know Mamá has insulted his pride.

"Could you please leave all the bad things and the bad words out when you tell them your story?" Mamá wants him to leave out the sex adventures in the *burdeles*. "Woman, I tell my children my story the way it is. They can handle it. They know it is the past." I know Papá is trying to get us to understand his story in his own language. For some of us, what he tells us piques our curiosity, as we imagine him young, in *pachuco* pants with a red shirt and shiny charcoal black shoes. We imagine him dancing mambo, but I don't allow myself to imagine the faces of the women in the stories, as I feel I would be betraying Mamá.

Papá begins one story: " 'You, son of a bitch, aren't you a fucking *Santaneco*?' The *Sonsonateco* man wields a machete to me. The *finca's* men are resentful of the *caporales'* warm reception to me, a man from Santa Ana. I am in a finca in Sonsonate. I roll up my sleeves. 'What did you say, son of a bitch? Do you want me to beat you up, sissy boy?' I say with a stick in my hand. 'Demetrio, don't fight this guy,' the caporal advises me."

Papá also at one time had his name as Demetrio, and changed it himself (before he met Mamá) to Antonio according to his favorite Saint, San Antonio Del Monte.

"'What *puta* gave birth to you that you call me *hijo de puta*?'

68

"The man raises his machete to strike me. I grab a pole with a machete blade wired to its end, slash the man across his stomach, and I run away. The police find me hiding in a chicken coop. They imprison me in the village of El Tepecoyo in the department of Sonsonate. After two months in jail, my friend, Miguel, pays my bail of fifteen *colones*. Afterwards, Miguel introduces me to a well-connected man named Macario who builds houses and furniture out of cement. Macario is very rich and a little strange, as he hires only men who earn his trust. 'Well, boy, I want you to bathe my woman,' Macario tells me as he considers hiring me. I have never touched a naked woman before. Her name is María Elena. She is as ugly as La Siguanaba when she reveals her true identity to men. I wash her body with a loofa sponge and Camay soap. She has nice olive skin, and a body shaped like a pear. Her face is ugly, though. In order to get this good job in construction, María Elena has to approve of each apprentice. I pour water on her feet, then on her hair. I ask her to sit in the chair in order to pour it over her head. She is just a little taller than me. I do not even think about her body. Instead, I dream about construction and houses. I tell María Elena that, when I get married, I want to build a house for my wife and children. María Elena likes my long speeches. She takes my hand, puts it over her voluminous left breast and says, 'You will have your house and wife. My husband, Macario, will teach you construction.' "

Papá gets up to pick up a shovel, a bag of cement, and a water bucket. It is as though he is gathering the ingredients to cook up something, even as he continues talking to us, his children. Then in a wheelbarrow with sand and gravel, he shows us how to mix all these important ingredients to build a wall. He mixes and churns in seconds the ingredients into the concrete mixture. By this time, the littlest one escapes to play and to ask Mamá for something to eat. Silently he pours the wheelbarrow full of concrete into the trench just behind us where he had laid out some rebar the day before.

"One morning Macario wakes me up to tell me that I do not have to wash his woman anymore. 'Boy, get ready, we're going to buy you new clothes and shoes.' I get up fast and splash water on my face. My clothes are all worn out. It's a Saturday and he takes me to a clothing store. 'Get those shoes there. They are Benny Moré style, you know, the Mambo King. And those pants over there, the *pachuco* pants.' I tuck in my new satin shirt and leather belt. Macario laughs. I leave the store looking like I'm in a mambo band."

"'Let's go. Today you'll be a man. I'll take you first to *Los Claros de Luna* to learn to dance mambo. Then, I'll take you to a *burdel*. You know what a *burdel* is? There's one of the best here in Sonsonate, *El Janeiro de la Monchona*.' I heard the word *burdel* before from Miguel. It's the place where Miguel fell in love with Mensol. She's the woman who eventually caused him to leave me behind."

Papá says the last words quivering slightly, stands up, puts his arms together, then clasps his hands, as though he is going to pray for his friend to appear. We few brothers and sisters who have not wandered off and who remain together, some of us with our mouths half-opened, look at each other. We are searching and scanning one another with impatient eyes, trying to think up words to cut the silence. We have been possessed by the lost, dramatic, and impenetrable silence Papá has taken on.

I think I can predict how he's going to continue the story. He will look up at the blue sky, let loose a big sigh, sniffle a little, and sit and place both his hands on the hard cement floor and tell us, "You do not know what cold is, what hungers is, what escaping is, what to live without a roof is." But no, I am wrong. This time he says, "This silence is in honor of and respect for Miguel, my friend, my family, and my childhood." Then Papá clears his throat drinks a little from the barrel of rainwater, and passes to us the same plastic container that we use to bathe to drink from too. He sits down again to continue the story.

"'I don't have any money, sir. How can I pay for the dances?' I say to Macario. 'Don't worry, Demetrio. Next week you'll pay me by working in construction.' 'But I don't know construction.' 'You'll learn fast, Demetrio. Do you know how to dig holes in the dirt?' 'Yes. Also I know how to count to one hundred, and I recognize numbers. Also I can measure the distance by looking at the moon and the sea.' 'Boy, today you'll measure women. And next week the nails.' "

My older sister, Estela, reacts to these last two sentences, telling Papá, "That man was bad." I thought about the words too, about how Papá pronounced both "women" and "nails" with the same enthusiasm. I join Estela in her protest. Papá quickly readjusts himself placing a finger to his lips, as he sees us getting up to run out. "Do you want to know how it happened or not? I am not telling you lies like other fathers tell their children to think they have been good all their lives. This is the raw story of how I became a construction master." Estela and I manage to recognize the sincerity in his eyes. "Continue then," we say in chorus, my brothers and sister, affirming and nodding, too. "Pay attention, and open your ears," he says touching his moustache.

"It's in *Janeiro de la Monchona* that I learn how to dance *mambo, rumbas, los porros* along with the music of Beny Moré and Perez Prado. I especially remember my first tango. I danced with this beautiful woman of *la vida alegre*. I learn *El Mambo Azul*, and Macario was proud that I learned to be a good dancer. The owner called me *Pachuco*. Every Saturday we went to dance and meet women. From Macario I learned to say, '*Vamos al puerto libre*,' where you are allowed to do anything you want with a woman without feeling guilty or having to act like a gentleman. I learned many things quickly."

"Macario is a drunk and eventually he puts me in charge of all his construction sites. I pick him up off the streets, when he gets so drunk he isn't able to make it home on his own. I feed him and give him a little alcohol in the morning to cure his hangover. I get tired of his nightmares. He dreams again and again the devil is taking him away, carrying him through the canyons among the volcanoes. He dreams *el Diablo* is sleeping with his mother, who died before he was ten years old. We lose that construction job eventually, when Macario can't even manage the small and easy details that are his to do. I put two hundred *colones* in his pocket one morning, but before I leave him, I ask him the name of the engineer he keeps mentioning, the one he dreamed of working with again. I memorize the name: Sebastian Ardón. 'Everyone knows him in the city,' he says. That's how I left for the capital."

"In 1950, I arrive in San Salvador. The smell of the city and the lights of the cars awaken a dream in my soul, a dream I had

71

since I was a child, a dream that smells like a modern home with modern cooking. The dream smells of construction, bricks, and cement. It smells of bursting wild herbs and ripe coffee, of flowers and guava trees in bloom around me. I tell myself I am ready for the city. Even though the speed of life in the capital causes me some nausea, I say to myself, 'Who cares?' I know I am from volcanoes and trees, where my feet only touch real soil, not cement. For a little while anyway, the city makes me feel a little dizzy, like the first time I went fishing on a boat. I think it might have come from not knowing anyone in the city. But Sebastian Ardón fills all my senses from the moment I step off the bus at the *Terminal Occidental* at seven o'clock in the morning."

"I am supposed to take city bus number seven, I think, to *el parque* Libertad where I heard Macario mention there are men who gather to look for work. They also trade things on the black market. 'Be careful of thieves!' Macario's voice echoes through my mind. But since I have fought with the strongest men in the countryside, I feel sure the capital will be easier."

"When I get off the bus, I see a beautiful cathedral, and many other grand monumental buildings around the city. I walk toward the cathedral and touch it as though it is a woman. I try to take in all the lines and curves, which, in reality, don't have anything to do with the curves of women I have touched, but I feel how everything is built of metal and with wood. I see emerald as a color for the first time. I want to build something like this one day. I do not understand how to measure, or design, nor even to read, but I know I can learn to build like this. I stay in *el parque* Libertad observing everything. By eleven o'clock in the morning, I am in the cathedral kneeling and praying to the Virgin Maria and Jesus to guide me to the engineer Ardón. The cathedral is almost empty and full of silence. I spend hours inside the cathedral."

"When I go out into the street, the smell and smoke of the buses and cars penetrates my brain, causing me to feel off-balance. I am so dizzy I almost fall. I feel for a moment as though I am being swallowed into a dark hole by a countryside night. Suddenly a ray of light with the illuminated face of *El Salvador Del Mundo* descends from heaven. Jesus' face is already so familiar to me, but now it's more like a woman's face. Perhaps she is the Virgin I saw in the cathedral, or maybe it is my Mamá. She talks to me, and tells me that it is not my time to die."

"I realize it is already late evening and I have not eaten all day. The smell of my mother's food comes back to me. I was only five years old the last time I smelled her food—cooked rice in lard with tomatoes and onions with a small piece of grilled chicken. Months later Mamá died and I was all alone. My brothers, sisters, and I were all handed out to relatives. That's another story."

"The darkness and the smell disappear with a touch on my arm. *La señora*, the seller of rosaries and *camándulas*, asks whether I'm feeling all right. I walk to *el parque* Libertad, but now the streetlights are on. I sit down on the cement edge that borders the water fountain. Children are playing. Women walk around. I am still wearing the clothes Macario bought me. A small, nice-looking young woman with beautiful hips sits down next to me. From across the park I see a man watching me. I walk away from that spot, leaving the young woman by herself. I do not want trouble in a place where I do not know how this kind of thing works. I walk to the gates in front of *el parque* Libertad to study the construction of the arches. The man who was staring at me starts following me. 'Where are you from?' he has silver-crowned front teeth. 'From El Barrio Candelaria.' I only mention this place because I heard Miguel talking about it. 'You are not from there. Do not lie.' The man moves quickly to my side as though he wants to talk in secrets. Then, once he is close to me he whispers, 'Are you a *chivo*?' I say, 'I am not. I do not mix with prostitutes to manage them either. I am a builder.' 'But you are not from the city?' 'Yes sir, you are right. I am not from here. I just arrived this morning.' 'Have you come here to escape from something?' he asks as though he already knows the answer. A siren silences the moment. 'No, sir.' I affirm to him. 'My name is Justino,' he says. 'I am Antonio, once called Demetrio, but I am baptized now as Antonio, like San Antonio Del Monte who has always done miracles and favors for me.'

'Boy, you look like you're a good soul' 'I am, sir, and I am a
good worker.' 'In that case, you should change those clothes, as
you look like a pimp with those shiny red shoes, yellow satin
shirt and your pants, *pachuco*. That's why that girl there got so
close to you. She thought you were a pimp. I've slept with her.
She is quite expensive. I like her a lot but she would not leave
this life. I am a plumber myself.' 'I am looking for an engineer
named Ardón.' I was hoping he might recognize the name.
While I'm adjusting my belt and tucking in my shirt better, he
says 'Do you have a place to stay?' 'No, sir, I was planning to
sleep here, in the corner by the doorway.' 'I know the engineer
you're talking about.' Something about this man makes me trust
him: the hammer, the measurement tape attached to his waist
belt, and his hands. When I shake his hand, they feel calloused,
the hands of an honest construction worker. They have soul, a
wandering soul, like mine, but I do not like his silver teeth. I do
not trust men with silver teeth."

"'You do? You know engineer Ardón? Can you take me to him
tomorrow?' I say this, drawing close to him as though we are
sharing a secret. 'Come with me. I have a place not far from
here.' He runs his right hand over his curly short hair. For some
minutes, I walk behind him. He's taller than me. I am sure I will
grow more, since I am only nineteen years old. We take a bus to
a place called Antiguo Cuscatlán. He says he lives in a *mesón*
called *La Flecha* with his blind mother. It is a cardboard house. I
sleep on the even, clean, dirt floor. Justino's mother tells him in
a soft voice, almost whispering like a small creek running
through ravines, to give me the warm white cotton blanket. A
plastic curtain separates his mother's room from his. Justino is a
strong-boned, big-chested thirty-year-old, with a gaunt face and
few hairs growing from his chin. He looks older than his age."

"All night I pray to San Antonio Del Monte to locate engineer
Ardón , so he can offer me a job tomorrow. Eventually I hope to
meet a girl different from the ones I have met at the *burdeles*. I
can't sleep. I feel the darkness of the little house and listen to
Justino's snoring, which sounds like the tide as it drags back and
forth on black rocks, or maybe like the scraping of a pan. The
mother asks for something around three o'clock in the morning. I
know it has to be three in the morning because the roosters are

starting to crow. Hearing them in the darkness I feel exactly as I had in my childhood bed and the memory is as sweet to me as a glass of raw milk. I thought I'd hidden my memories from myself so they could never be obstacles to my continuing my life as the orphan I am."

"I think about my brother, Lucio, and my sisters, who were sent to stay with different people. I pray to *El Niño De Atocha* that I will see them again. Lucio stayed with Grandma after Mamá died. A few months later my father was killed. I also stayed with grandma Isabel, but she was so mean, she burned my hair because I ate an extra tortilla. I was seven years old. The roosters' call weighs heavy, like a cement rock on my chest. I don't get up. I pretend I am sleeping. I cry in silence. Lucio will look for me some day, or I'll find him, my older brother."

"Justino's mother starts making hissing sounds. Justino takes her outside where the baño is. They pass me. I am covered from head to toe with the blanket. I must look like a sack of flour. The blanket smells like firewood smoke. I am sure that like my mother, Justino's mother saves her things under her bed or in the kitchen. The moment I see Justino walking so patiently with his mother, I understand that he is a good man. I trust him completely."

"At six in the morning, Justino makes a breakfast of fried beans, eggs, corn coffee and toasted tortillas on the *comal*. He serves his mother on his bed. He and I eat in the kitchen standing up. 'Ready?' Justino's voice is raspy and melodic at the same time. 'For what?' I ask adjusting my belt. 'To meet the engineer you are here for.' He gulps the last drops of his coffee. 'I am completely ready, my friend,' I say. I am quite determined. We leave the house at quarter to seven in the morning. An orange morning greets us when we get out into the street. The smell outside is the same as my blanket, like the soul of these houses smells of firewood. People, mostly men, walk to get the bus. I guess that like me, they hope to find a job, or someone to give them a day's work."

"By ten o'clock, I think Justino must have lied about knowing the engineer Ardón. We visit construction site after construction site, and each time, Justino tells me to wait for him while he approaches the men to ask for the engineer. He returns each time saying in his rasping voice something like: 'They say he just left for another site.' I finally sit down on a cement block beside one construction site, still feeling the morning's breakfast turning in the pit of my stomach. 'Are you lying to me? You do not know him, do you?' Justino stands up very straight and looks like he wants to fight me. Just when I think he is going to hit me, I see a young man carrying bricks on a cart toward the construction site where we had just been. The cart hits a rock in the road, and all the bricks fall off the cart so I run to help him. 'Thank you, boy,' says the friendly young man. I tell him, 'I am not a boy, I am nineteen. I am a young man like you.' But I ask, 'Do you know an engineer named Sebastian Ardón?' 'Yes, he's here. Are you looking for work?' I say a silent 'thank you' to San Antonio Del Monte. 'Yes, I am,' I say gratefully. 'Stand up, boy. We need somebody who can lay brick fast. I know a maestro who works with Señor Ardón. Come with me. He might hire both of you.' "

"'My name is Antonio-once-Demetrio,' I say shaking his hand. 'I am Gabriel.' He talks slowly and wipes the sweat off his forehead with the back of his hand. The morning is burning off its cool air.' 'This is Justino,' I say. 'He is also looking for work.' 'I can find my own work, peasant boy,' Justino says. His resentment is cold as stone. Then he walks away. Gabriel gestures for me to follow him to meet the engineer. From a distance I yell 'thank you' many times to Justino, off whose strong back and broad shoulders my gratitude bounces indifferently right back at me. I remained in the area of El Pueblo Antiguo Cuscatlán."

Mamá is back and calls Estela and me to help her with some chore. "Did you ever see Justino again?" I ask before I go to Mamá. "I never saw him again. Later I learned from Gabriel that he already knew Justino. He said, even though Justino was a friend to you for that one night, eventually he would have made you pay for that kindness in a strange way." Estela and I run fast to help Mamá, but she just wants us to bring a tray outside for us to eat tortillas, cheese and avocado, with fresh lemonade. We love that way she does it, a little salt on the tortillas and avocados and not too much sugar in the lemonade. It is so good, and so we can continue listening to Papá, our entertainer.

"When Gabriel leads me to him and I meet Sebastian Ardón, the engineer simply tells me to start working. I want to tell him how I came from far away to meet and work for him. Instead, I just walk behind Gabriel, my stomach still cramping from my nervousness at finally meeting the engineer. I join the other working men. Gabriel and I start mapping out the area where the bricks will go. We take turns mixing the mortaring cement and transporting the bricks. The sun falls hot on my head. I begin setting the bricks alongside the master bricklayer, who is also only a boy a little older than me. He is long and skinny, and so the men call him 'Escalera.' By the end of the day I have helped Escalera Gabriel lay about eight hundred bricks."

"I don't feel the length of this first day. I don't eat lunch. The few words I utter have to do with construction. I want to observe the engineer, who is busy directing the men at work. Gabriel says there is a lot of work for Ardón over the next few months and I will have more than enough time to see him. I don't have time to listen to the jokes that make the other workers laugh as they throw kisses to the girls and women who come to sell them food and drinks. That first night I stay at Gabriel's house. When he realizes I don't have a place to stay, he takes me to his house where I meet all his family."

"By the end of the second week we get paid. I buy work shoes, pants, and a shirt, and pay some money to Gabriel's mother. My life is now construction work. After a few months of proving that I'm a hard worker and a good learner, the engineer Ardón asks me to work for him at other constructions sites. He shows me the blueprints of the properties and how to measure all aspects of the land we're building on. 'You boy, I like you, because you pay attention, even though you don't know how to read. You observe, and you listen.' Ardón says this, as he hands me a new tape measure, a hammer, and a box of colored pencils I'll use to note my measurements. My friend, Gabriel, is not at all resentful of my success and advancement in the construction business. He is happy for me and proud of me. He tells me, 'But be careful, as there are some men here who are jealous about your new position close to Señor Ardón.' "

"In the *pueblo* and at my construction job I make three friends: Santos, Carlos, and Gabriel. Carlos and Santos play *Marimba* in the village park every Sunday, and I often accompany them. Sometimes in the evenings after work we walk around the *salones de baile* in the pueblo or play poker with Gabriel. I meet girls in these dance halls, but none of them can be my wife. I keep the clothes Macario bought me as my dancing attire and Sunday wardrobe. Gabriel tells me that the celebration of Corpus Christi, a big celebration, with bands and free food is coming to the church of *el pueblo*."

Papá at a distance looks over at the temporary house where Mamá is, and somehow his face glows as though lit in a morning sun. With a smile, he then gets up and quickly runs to where Mamá is standing. His hands hold her face as he tries to kiss her. Mamá pushes him away, as she does not like to be kissed in front of his kids. "Go. They are waiting for you to finish your story."

"On a Sunday in 1951, I walk into the Corpus Christi celebration in the park of Antiguo Cuscatlán just to take a look around, to see what they have. I listen to the music, and I see my friends who play *Marimba*. There are hanging *piñatas* on display shaped into all kinds of animal figures, and they are full of bright, beautiful pink, orange, yellow, blue, white tissue paper."

"I dance Mambo in the park. Without thinking, I glance at a table with girls handing out drinks. I sigh enchanted. It is a sigh I never experienced before in my nineteen years. I see this one very beautiful girl. She's very young, but she looks like the leader of the group, even though she is probably the youngest of all the girls. I stare at her long straight brown hair, light skin, almond-shaped brown eyes, the pink of her cheeks and her tiny waist. She is wearing high-heeled shoes with red heels and a red dress that falls to her knees. She only smiles when necessary. She seems very serious as she serves the *horchata*. I walk over to the table. '*Chelita*, would you give me an *horchata*?' I smile, trying not to offend her with any gesture or body movement. I am trying to think of what I can promise her to be my wife. She serves me and says, 'Do not call me *Chelita*. And we all know, the girls here, that you have been observing us from a distance.' I slip a little on a banana leaf that has fallen from the table to the ground. I almost lose my balance as I am getting close to her. I pull myself together. The girls laugh. 'I was only observing you. What is your name?' I say in a voice that seems to be coming out

78

from another being. But it is me. I am in front of her. 'No one gives me my name. I call myself Altagracia.' She gives me back my smile. 'Would you like to go with me tonight to the dance at City Hall?' 'I do not go dancing,' she says and her tone is even more serious than it was when she served me the *horchata.* 'Do you live close by?' I ask hoping she will say she is from around here. There is a short silence. 'I am working--- please leave me alone.' 'You will be the mother of my children,' I say looking her in the eye. 'You are crazy. You are saying nonsensical things.' She starts serving other people, but she turns to watch me as I leave. I step behind the big *ceiba* tree in the middle of the park, and pray in silence 'San Antonio del Monte, please save this beautiful angel, so that she might become my wife. I feel like a fool. I feel I am growing inside and outside like this fat tree I am leaning on.

"Later that night I go dancing with Gabriel and tell him about this girl whose name is Altagracia. I was hoping he might know her. He laughs, 'She is my first cousin and she's only fourteen years old. Her name is really Rosa Maria Melida, not Altagracia, but ever since she was small, she's wanted everyone to call her by that name. I don't know why. She says she has dreams with that name. Hey, she is my favorite cousin, so be careful.' Gabriel laughs as he rolls up his white cotton sleeves, exposing his strong arms."

"Within six months after arriving in this *pueblo*, all my wishes come true. By the time of the coffee harvest, my worries about the jealousy of other men falls away like the first fight I had in Sonsonate. I wish I could see Macario to tell him about working with Sebastian Ardón and to let him know what a good man and a good engineer he is, just as Macario described him. My greatest hope for Macario is that he has not died from drinking. I want to show him my calloused hands from working hard in construction. And I want to tell him about Altagracia, the girl, the woman, who will one day be the mother of my children."

There is something melancholic and victorious in Papá's gesture as he finishes his story. He tells us, "Go play now, you are free." Then he disappears among the bushes and the mango trees. My brothers and sisters and I, the ones who stayed until the end, go to ask Mamá for more food. Something different is happening to me this time after listening to the story. I think about their first smiles, Papá's and Mamá's, when they first met. I feel still suspended this time by his story. I look at the unfinished mansion he has been building. Did Mamá and he plan this mansion together when they met?

Later in the afternoon, I write a story for Papá and Mamá. I leave it in the notebook under my bed. One day, I'll read it for them.

...after...CAROLINA RIVERA ESCAMILLA

Altagracia

"I do not like the name my mamá Paula gave me at birth. I used to mix the original name with imagined ones, like cooking up recipes. At other times, I tried to pair names as I do with my shoes and clothes to see whether they fit me. And sometimes I would wear the names, depending on my mood. My original name is Rosa Maria---an ugly name, a name from a *cumbia*, and *cumbia* music is not my thing. Perhaps if the names had the taste of *boleros*, I would have used them, but 'Rosa Maria is so common in the mouth of men,' I told my mamá."

"They have called me by all these names: María Melida, Rosa Melida, or Rosa María, but my sisters, my brother, and even my father, all call me *la Chele*, white like milk or *leche* said backwards. When I met your Papá, I told him I call myself Altagracia, as this is a name I like. I dreamed it. Now, you, sons and daughters, have known me with all these names until now. Before I leave our house today to get married, you should know this: I'm happy that people have been confused about my names. Until I turned fourteen, I said my name was Altagracia. It is the name I asked my sister Queta to stitch into the border of my white linen handkerchiefs my mamá used to buy for me, so I could wipe the sweat from my face on hot humid days and whenever I walked from house to house offering quesadilla cakes on weekends. Why did I like to call myself Altagracia?"

"My Grandma Chana worked for years to raise her children by baking and selling quesadillas. I used to observe Grandma Chana as she mixed fine rice flour, sugar, sour cream, and eggs, and then she would bring out a spoonful of yeast that she said would make the squared quesadilla moist and grow in the baking pan. My mamá, Paula, joined her mother in the quesadilla baking, as soon as she lost the job at the colonial's house."

"By then I had told my mamá that Altagracia was the name I had dreamed about. In my dream I was able to see three parallel roads on a slope of mounded earth. The upper road looked like long black hair held in place with rows of shiny green, blue and violet combs. On the middle road a group of women held candles as they walked slowly in the opposite direction of the flow of the long hair, along a part in the scalp where green combs swayed. The third road was for me and my four sisters, Queta, Lina, Mati, and Yita. I saw myself walking in front of my sisters, who were laughing and pointing at the waves of hair, that now turned emerald greens and blues, like the colors in feathers on peacocks, like the ones I had seen in the zoo where my Papá had taken me. Hidden behind the long hair someone screamed the name 'Altagracia, Altagracia.' My sisters stopped laughing, and I heard echoes of someone calling their names. In front of me a tall ladder appeared with each step of the ladder made of an emerald green comb. Engraved on each step was the name 'Altagracia.' I ran to take a comb-step, but the ladder disappeared for a moment and then reappeared extending hands to hold each of my hands. As I took a hand in each of mine, I felt that they were the hands of Mamá and Papá. It seemed the hands were blowing on the candles. As they did this, the hands also spoke the name 'Altagracia.' "

"I had the same dream many times. The next time the shining green emerald comb emerged from a cave and called me to go inside to help dig her out. The third time I dreamed this dream, there was the long ladder with her black hair. The ladder was lying down on the road laughing and saying 'Altagracia is my name, but now I baptize you Altagracia.' Then my sisters appeared all in yellow dresses and Queta with her big brown eyes smiling at me, said, 'You are *La* Chele, *La* Chelita, because your dad is El Chele, lucky you, lucky you,' she laughed."

"Another time in the dream I am picked up by a red butterfly and carried by the wind. The floating butterfly was screaming 'Altagracia, Altagracia.' This was the first time Mamá and Yita found me in the bed screaming the name Altagracia."

"I started having these dreams when I was nine years old, and Mamá and Papá had already separated by circumstances I was not supposed to know about, and you children are not allowed yet to know or ask about those circumstances either."

"At seven years old I started to learn how to sell the baked quesadilla that my grandmother and Mamá had baked under the mud oven that turned a pomegranate color when its embers were hottest. Papá had built the oven in the patio before he left. I would talk to passersby, who would say to me, 'Chelita, sell me half a quesadilla, que linda Chelita.' People would tell me this as they passed by our house, whether there were quesadillas to sell or not. 'My name is Altagracia,' I would tell them in all seriousness standing in a heavily starched dress. I took and counted their money, and put it in the apron with just one long pocket across it. The people laughed at me, but in the end they started calling me Altagracia. 'It is true that you have grace, and you are a gracious child,' people would say in front of me, and even Yita admitted I was very beautiful. 'You are the most beautiful child in this pueblo, not only because you are beautiful, but because you are chele white, like the white rose, and we are all brown like the baked quesadillas.' Yita always says she is African like her father."

"'Do not waste this girl, Paula. Send her to school. With that skin color she can marry very well,' the neighbors offered advice. Mamá did not want me to work in the coffee grove, or to clean the Colonia Master's houses within the pueblo, as my sisters did for Señor or Don Walter Deninger. Walter Deninger asked my mamá many times to 'send La Chelita to my house. She can come to feed the white *ganzos* and the peacocks and pick the roses and other flowers. I will send her to school.' He would leave a package of cookies at my Mamá's feet. Mamá wished she had money so she could stop my sisters and my brother from working for him. We moved away from the *colonos*, because Mr. Walter Deninger kept begging Mamá to give me away to him to work in his house and to travel with him and his wife to Germany. When my mamá said no, he felt insulted. I was standing there, listening, looking up at the white-skinned German, with his irritating voice, like one of his screaming white geese. He turned his tomato-red face at my Mamá. 'You're a stupid woman. Don't you see I am trying to make your daughter something? She deserves to be something; she is beautiful' When he would touch my skin, or my hair, Mamá would take his hand off me and push the German man out of the house. 'Paula, stop what you're doing. He's right. Give La Chele to him. Otherwise, she will end up marrying one of those *indios cabrones campesinos*. There's nothing good in this pueblo,' Esteban would say to Mamá. 'Why are you helping this man?' Mamá would fire back. Esteban was my sister, Mati's boyfriend and husband-to-be."

"'I want all of you out of this house by tomorrow," Mr. Walter Deninger made it terribly obvious to Mamá the last time he left the house. 'And you do not have work with me anymore.' I cried. The German man left the house, his face bulging like an overly ripe tomato. My sisters, brother, and soon-to-be brother-in-law all got mad at Mamá and blamed me, because we were forced out of the colonos house. Mamá took the important things and folded them inside a big blanket, and did the same thing for my sisters. Yita was already thirteen. Mamá went to rent a room in a mesón where we all lived--- Queta, Lina, Manuel, Yita and me. The only ones who stayed on with Don Walter were Esteban and Mati, who claimed they were a family unrelated to Mamá. Eventually, Manuel, Lina and Queta got their own rooms and lived with their girlfriend and boyfriends. Soon they got their jobs back with Don Walter Deninger. They were not punished because they were hard workers, and Manuel told Mr. Deninger that, 'Our Mamá is a good mother, but I do not know why she is so protective of La Chele, since La Chele's father is not even of good breeding. He is twisted in his mind. We call him El Chele. He claims to speak to the devil, and to have a pact with him. Under the ceiba tree, when he's drunk, El Chele cries and asks the devil to return his love, and we do not know what love he's talking about. La Chele is a special girl. She is beautiful and white, but she is always dreaming weird things. You know, Mr. Deninger, La Chele and Yita, are half-sisters to us, to Lina, Queta, Mati and me, but we love them as full sisters, because half their blood is from our Mamá, whose husband, our father, died long ago. But El Chele was a hardworking man. I do not know why he had to run away from el pueblo. To tell you the truth, Señor Deninger, I wanted to kill him, because he did something that we can't talk about, but our Mamá was very hurt by it, and, for a while, she did not even care about me killing him, but La Chele was there, and Mamá did not want the little girl to be scared of me and hate me forever.' 'I remember El Chele as a good worker,' Mr. Deninger stated without looking at Manuel. Then he complained, 'Your mother is a stubborn woman. The little girl is such a beautiful virgin. What a waste! Crazy woman, your mother.' "

"Manuel started getting his fists ready to hit Mr. Deninger, but he knew he needed to keep the job. So instead, he hit his chest. No one has ever spoken badly about Mamá. Manuel had beaten El Chele, my papá, because he had done something that disrespected Mamá. I did not know what my papá did to Mamá, but Manuel did not want to see him around her or me. All these things I pieced together, as I grew up, from everything I heard in the family."

"Mamá did send me to school when I turned seven years old. She sent me to learn sewing, too, in Victoria's house. Victoria bought or made me the most beautiful dresses made of expensive cotton and chiffon, the kind of dresses actresses wore. 'That's what you deserve, Chelita,' she used to say. She became my godmother. Mamá trusted her. She cooked *godornizas sudadas*, something like wild duck with honey. She fed me, but she always asked me to try to connect with people from the other world."

"Mamá took me out from Victoria's house, when I started to be sick all the time. One day, when she came to pick me up, she found me in bed. Victoria was dressed with a cotton white dress, barefoot, and a red handkerchief on her head, a brown fat cigar between her lips, standing in front of the bed, then she kneeled down praying with lit candles, saints, and smoke from plants that she believed could bring back the spirits of the dead all around me. She murmured unfamiliar language, and getting me to play with a Ouija board, because she said I had special channels to communicate with the other world. Victoria asked me not to tell anyone, because people from the other world would come and set her house on fire with a strange fire, just like the spirits that would attack the neighbors' house. Victoria said that the neighbors' house would catch fire at night, and the whole family, mother, husband, and children became like wild hogs with large white canines, heavily furred ears, and black rough skin like the winter nights and they would come to steal her food, and they would attack anyone walking by their home. I had heard stories about that family from other people, but I never saw it. I never talked to these neighbors, since they never talked to anyone either."

"Also there was Victoria's boyfriend or husband, who was also my godfather, a young man, who claimed not to have any family. She used him, too, as a medium to the other world. Victoria took people inside her house. She was known to be very generous. No one realized that she was generating money, supposedly helping people in the pueblo to connect through my godfather and me with their loved ones who had passed away. I started getting sick. I was getting paler and felt nauseous every time I tried to eat. I was only nine years old. Mamá said she thought that maybe the red old man was coming already into my life, referring to possible symptoms of menstruation. Yita looked at me suspiciously, as though I was behaving this way to get extra attention, by stealing her time with Mamá. 'La Chele needs your attention all the time, Mamá.' Mamá thought that perhaps Yita was giving me tobacco, since she had started working at the tobacco farm, where she became addicted to smoking. We even used to go together to find cigarette butts on the ground around the cantinas in the pueblo. We only picked up the half-smoked ones. 'You're dirty. You're going to be sick," I would whisper to her.

In the afternoons, when we were left alone, Yita managed to make her cigarettes with the dry tobacco leaves. She smoked and then went to sit in the patio swing, where she whistled very melancholic sounds like a song, and asked me to swing her. But instead I spun and spun her around. She laughed, sometimes vomited and would run inside the house to rinse her mouth and to drink water and then fall sleep. When Mamá came home from work, she asked me what was happening to Yita? I told her, 'Yita ate tobacco, Mamá.' Mamá would wake Yita up, whose hair was crazy curly and almost always tousled. Coming out to the kitchen, Yita would complain, 'Chele *mentirosa*, you little white liar. You're the sick little girl. Do not believe her, Paula. She is lying. She talks in a strange language when she's asleep. Liar.' Yita called our mother by her first name, and only rarely called her Mamá. I never did that. I always knew them that way, more like a relationship between sisters, not like a mother and daughter. Yita was tiny, skinny, with beautiful curls, when she took the time to groom her hair. Her hair adorned her oval soft brown face. But I think she was born sad and angry. Mamá bought her dresses and she always gave them to me."

"The last time Mamá entered Victoria's house, that is, before Victoria could hide all her secret stuff about the other world, she was like a burst of wind pushing open the door. I was in bed trying to invoke a dead person Victoria had asked me to communicate with. Mamá was tiny and thin like Yita, but that day she carried me in her arms, where I felt sheltered in giant soft dove wings."

"That day I started selling *quesadillas* with her. She left her job in the coffee groves. Yita went to work in the coffee groves and on the weekends she sold tomatoes in the Central Market. 'Gracias, Paula, for letting me go to work, so I don't have to stay home with La Chele.' 'I am Altagracia. I beg you not to call me Chele.' "

"'You see Paula, she believes her name is Altagracia, not Rosa. Sometimes she calls herself Melida, but Altagracia for sure. She even dreams with that name,' Yita was shaking her head and scratching it at the ends of her phrases. She sounded tired. 'She is crazy. Victoria made her travel into other worlds.' Altagracia responded, 'Well, you hide cigarette butts in your hair.' "

"'Yita, be quiet...let her name herself whatever she wants. If she likes Altagracia, let her to play with the name,' Mamá says already grinding beans on the stone."

"Today, on this February day in 1976, with eleven children born, and the twelfth within me, your father and I are finally getting married officially before a judge, and I have to give my legal name: Rosa Maria. It is hard for me, children, to say this name. And at last, we will figure out how to fix your Papá's name. But that's another story. Let's go."

...after...CAROLINA RIVERA ESCAMILLA

Casas de Cartón/Cardboard Houses

"Sh, sh, quiet! He's fallen asleep. He is very weak. Look at his face...all cut up. This time they didn't just make fun of him... they almost killed him!"

Maria sits at the side of the bed, relieved that Octavio is finally unconscious, no longer bothering anyone. The weight of her body rests on the cold metal bed frame and pushes the thin foam mattress. The bedsprings squeak like a dozen disturbed mice. She stands quickly, heading toward the door. "Come on, go to sleep, everyone," Maria says in a soft voice as she shoos away the neighbors.

"What happened? What's all this, Maria? Did he cut himself?" Some of them feign concern as though they know nothing of what happened to Octavio. Maria insists, "Go. Move. It's late."

The neighbors go back inside their own cardboard houses that look like collages with different pieces pasted in abstract forms all over the exterior walls. "Poor Maria. How could she have had such a thing for a son? Before he grew up, everyone was so good to her." The houses seem to speak volumes, "*Pobre* Maria. *Pobrecita.*" Maria blows out the candle, almost spitting at it. She plods back inside her house, muttering "*Gente maldita.* "

"What are you doing up, woman?" Her husband, Esteban, arrives earlier than usual from work.

"I can't sleep," Maria answers, quickly dropping the black plastic sheet she has pulled from under the bed to cover the mess Octavio made. She moves quickly to the other side of the room to get her husband his usual cup of coffee. Maria stands in front of Esteban. "Take off that dirty shirt and go wash up. You look more tired, more than usual. I know I am. I think it's already past midnight." Maria tries to keep his attention away from where Octavio sleeps.

"What's all this mess? Who tore up my hat?" Esteban stoops to pick up the shreds and notices the melting wax candle on the tiny table. "This is what you've been doing, wasting all the candles while this faggot destroys the house?" Estebán pushes Maria aside.

90

"Leave him alone, please, Estebán. It's not his fault," Maria cries softly.

"You always defend this drunk, this filthy *maricón*. Well, after all, he is your own sin." Esteban throws Maria hard against the bed frame. "I can't stand being here with that...." Esteban shouts throwing his hands up in the air as he heads out the door, and slams it behind him.

Maria gets up, rearranges her hair, and holds the left side of her face. From the doorway she yells, "He's your son, too."

"Bring him a whore that can make him a man," Esteban yells losing himself in the darkness of the night.

"Ah God, what am I going to do?" Maria says as she rejoins the silent night. At the edge of the dirt street, she recalls Octavio in first grade; he went for two months only.

"Mamí, I don't want to go to school. The children call me girls' names, and the boys touch my butt."

"Don't listen to them, Octavio. Go with your sisters."

"They don't like to go with me, because the boys call me Octavia." Octavio's sisters, Tula and Pilar, hide from him at school. They were already pre-teens, but only in third grade. Octavio was nine when he started first grade. Tula and Pilar quit school when Octavio stopped. Octavio's brother, Ismael, never went to school. He works as a construction helper in the new military *colonia* that is being built on land directly behind the cardboard houses. Maria goes back inside the house, picks up a kitchen knife, and retakes her position at the edge of the dirt road.

She begins a slow wail, "He is a good child, always helping everyone here. Why don't you remember how good he is?" She stands with her feet apart, glaring. "Cleaning, cooking for you, taking care of the little ones. What are you looking at, evil people? Come out from your houses. I know you are looking at me from there." She directs herself to the house of a family with two daughters. "Yeah, you, you people, your daughters took my son, playing with him like a doll, dressing him like a girl. This curse he has is all your fault." She slumps down to the ground.

"Octavio! Octavio! Stay here with me!" his mother calls to him, but the nine-year-old doesn't want to stay home. He wanders a few houses away. "*Buenos días, Don* Victorio. It's a

91

beautiful morning." Octavio's eyes are bright and interested. "Hi, *muchacho*. Has your mom let you go out? Be careful how you walk...walk like a man. Don't put those tight pants on."

"I don't have any other clothes. I've been growing." Octavio answers, embarrassed.

"Ah, boy, it looks like you're looking for something else with your buttocks hanging out like that. Just don't go anywhere near those men over there. They'll tell you things or try to touch your buttocks." Octavio runs home.

Maria goes to Don Victorio's house. "Victorio, why did you joke like that with my boy, giving him alcohol, playing with his mind," Maria raises a fist.

Olivia had warned her, after Octavio turned eleven. "Ah, that boy, don't trust him, because I saw him just a while ago talking to Juan in the dark area against the back part of the house, where the bushes are so thick. They were moving and I heard some crying, so I didn't stay." Maria looks hard at Juan's house. "Juan, Juan, yeah, you're the one. I want everyone to know about that, you raped my son. You threatened to kill anyone who would say the truth. Come out, you bastard! I'm not afraid of your police uniform!" She rushes to Juan's house, kicking it, demanding that he come out.

She walks back to the road trembling as she tries to separate her hair from the tears streaming down her face. She uses the knife to cut away at the hair she cannot separate from her face. She screams, "All your fault... all your fault."

Candles are relit inside one of the houses. The dogs bark from close and far away. Maria hugs herself, nestling her head on her shoulders and arms. A door opens, and Olivia emerges with a candle in her hand.

"Maria...Maria...come inside...have you lost your mind?"

"I don't know. I don't know."

Olivia puts her arm over her shoulder, guiding her to the house. "I will wash your face so that this evil thing will come out from you."

The next morning cardboard houses come gradually to life. At seven o'clock the stove fires are lit. Women and children are carrying empty *cantaros*, as they head out of the settlement either to buy water from the rich neighbors who live on the other side of the big wall, or to head in the opposite direction to see if they can find a construction crew at work. The workers always let them use the water hose for free. Only Maria's and Octavio's house stays shut.

Inside nineteen-year-old Octavio wakes up, touches his face, smarting at its rawness. He glances at the pictures of Bruce Lee, Veronica Castro, Lucia Mendez and David Carradine that are glued to the cardboard wall. The pictures are from used magazines he collected from the houses where he and his mother worked as *sirvientes,* cleaning and cooking. On the wall is a Polaroid photo from the 1970s. It is the only picture he has of himself with his mother and his older brother Ismael. His Uncle Antonio had taken it when Octavio was about fifteen years old.

He looks at his mother and brother and says, "I love you, Mamí. I love you, Ismael." He reaches past the picture to lift a tiny square mirror off a small nail. It had cost him one colon. He looks at himself in the tiny mirror, finding the long scratch marks on his purplish and discolored cheek.

Maria is still in bed, on the other side of the plastic curtain that separates her "room" from Octavio's. She stares at the rusty corrugated metal roof, imagining for a moment that her prayer will shoot through her eyes cut through the roof, and fly to God. "It is Sunday, the seventh day of the week, the Lord Jesus' free day. Thank you, God." Sunday is only a half-day of work for her.

Silently Octavio pushes aside the curtain and sits on the edge of the bed, sipping water from a faded green plastic cup he has used for years.

"Maria, I am very sorry for what I did last night," he whispers. She looks up at him and places her hand, just above his knee. "I am proud of you, Octavio. You saved that little girl from being molested by those beasts!" She sighs loudly. "Maria, I am very angry with these people around here, tired of this life where everyone thinks it's all right to do whatever they want to others." He swallows the last of the water, gets up from the bed, and stretches his arms to fully wake up. His eyes settle on Esteban's *tombilla,* a round bamboo container about one meter tall standing in the corner. "So Esteban has left again because of me." He reaches over and picks up one of Esteban's hats, pulls at a loose thread on its rim, then places it on his head, "That *maricón* is not my son! He is your sin, Maria. You must have slept with another man!" They both laugh.

Maria says in a hoarse voice, "Esteban will never understand. He is too ignorant and foolish to accept you as his son, just the way you are. She raises her hand to cover her eyes. The sun has found one of the many holes in the cardboard walls.

"What I really hate is that I look like him!" Octavio says. "I wish he wouldn't come back. He doesn't help with anything around here anyway. The little money that he brings in....damn, I could get it myself." He tosses the hat at the *tombilla* in the corner, goes to his mother and gives her a big hug. He pulls her long black hair into a bun, tying it with a piece of black cloth. "He has no other family, no place else to go. He will die here with us, Octavio." Maria bends over to look at her feet, which are scraped up from kicking at Juan's house.

"Octavio, I had a fight last night, too." She rubs her feet, and with her gesture of the head indicates she wants the bottle of rubbing alcohol for her feet from the shelf. He hands the bottle to her.

"Who did you fight with, Maria? I didn't hear a thing."

"I fought with the wall of Juan's house." She laughs quietly, like a little girl. Octavio sits next to her and laughs too.

The neighbors have yet to say a word about what transpired the night before. Nonetheless, they have been communicating with one another through body language. Olivia stands in front of her house, which is the closest one to Maria's. She looks over at Maria's closed-up house, then toward the ever-strengthening sun, and wonders when there might be some sign of Maria and Octavio. The neighbors watch her in her distraction. She resumes the food preparation she always does after stacking the wood. Maria's house rings with soft laughter. Olivia smiles with relief.

Maria sits on an old brown wooden chair pushed against the wall, watching Octavio gesticulating as he recreates the night before. "I was drinking some beers with Juan's sons, and some other men. We all put our money together to go buy beer at Josefina's store. We were standing outside Josefina's drinking." He leans against the wall trying to look macho, an imaginary bottle in his hand. "I was getting very drunk, and I was saying how the *patrona* from my work wants to open up a store around here in our area... a food store."

Maria gets up from the chair. "It's getting late, Octavio. Let's talk after we get something to eat." They both move unconsciously in an almost synchronized ballet of movement to get coffee and reheated black beans and tortillas onto the table. They always work well together, usually in silence, as they clean houses or prepare food as *sirvientes* in the houses of various rich employers. By the time breakfast is ready, the door to their house is opened, the blinding bright sun acting as a barricade to their neighbors.

"I don't know what happened," says Maria. "I just know I heard Ana screaming, 'They're killing Octavio!' I came running and saw Juan's sons running away."

Ana is a neighbor Eva's daughter and has been working for Maria since she was five years old. Between bites of beans and tortillas she is already beginning the day's work. Maria pours a pound of uncooked red beans on the table, sorting out the gritty dirt or pebbles that are inevitably in the big sacks. She looks at the sacks of maize-corn on the floor against the wall, and Octavio picks, drags them toward the table. They will soon make fresh tortillas that Octavio and the ten-year old Ana deliver still warm house-to-house to the rich military families on the other side of the big wall at noon on Sundays in time for their dinner.

"You know, I really love Ana. We share our dreams whether they are nightmares or happy dreams. Although lately she has been having more nightmares than happiness dreams. What else can you dream living in this place? She calls me her big brother, and we would do anything for each other," Octavio says. "When I was drinking with the men in front of Josefina's store, Eva sent Ana over to buy cigarettes for her grandma. One of Juan's sons, Carlos, went over to her and said, 'Ana, what beautiful breasts you are growing!' They surrounded her and touched her, saying all kinds of disgusting things." Octavio grew flushed. "I told them, 'Leave her alone!' Carlos screams back at me, 'You *maricón*! What do you know about women?' The other men say, 'Are you jealous because you want us, Octavia? We can do you, too.' I broke into the circle, and smashed my bottle of beer over Carlos' head and grabbed Ana's hand. That's really the last thing

95

I remember clearly. I think one of them broke a bottle over my head. The next thing I remember was Ana helping me back to the house."

Maria gets up from the chair, "How many times have I told you to stay away from those beasts? How can you drink with them? They are criminals!"

"I'm sorry, Maria, for making a mess in the house last night." He looks forlorn.

"It's Sunday and it's already after nine o'clock. We have a lot of work to do to sell the tortillas."

Octavio steps outside to compose himself, and catches sight of Olivia. She is tying ribbons in the hair of the eldest of her two daughters. They are almost ready to go to church, wearing their white dresses. They will jump rope while their mother gets ready.

Olivia hurries toward Octavio, "*Buenos días*! or should I say *'Buenas tardes'* since you are getting up so late? How are you today?" Octavio avoids eye contact. "Those bastards beat me up last night!"

Olivia hesitates and turns around to go back home. Maria calls out to her, "Where are you going, Olivia?" Maria comes out of the house, goes up to Olivia and looks directly, softly into her face.

Olivia answers, "I'm going to the market to buy some fresh vegetables for the midday soup, and then if there's time we will go to church."

Maria affectionately taps Olivia on her shoulder. Olivia returns the simple touch and smiles at Maria. She looks back through the open door towards Octavio. Without raising his eyes from his tortillas, says, "Well, have a good day, then."

At noon Eva walks Ana to Maria's house. Octavio has been waiting for her to deliver the tortillas. Ana usually walks by herself to meet Octavio. Today she was a little afraid to go there by herself. Ana and Octavio always share their dreams and nightmares as they deliver the tortillas. One dream they both talk about often and can no longer remember whether they dreamed of it separately while asleep or whether they daydreamed it together out loud with constant embellishment is about losing their houses and land, the only thing they think they own. Ana and Octavio dream of a dust storm that shakes them out of their beds, of a volcano that spits an elongated metal shape like a bull. Its vertebrae are huge, and as the dust flies outward from it and gradually settles, there are revealed human-like machines with big horizontally and vertically wide mouths that snap at everything around as they dig and bury them alive with all their belongings under soft dark brown dirt. "It looks like a cemetery with no crosses or flowers," Ana says.

Ana is afraid of this dream but Octavio is not. He believes that dreams bring important messages and communicate something different from what the dream is. He says, "Dreams are in another language when one sleeps, foreign from our awakened speech." Ana feels comfortable with Octavio's understanding of dreams. She tells him that his interpretation of dreams feels like a pillow with soft feathers tenderly covering her ears. Octavio sighs and smiles, and tells her, "Perhaps that pillow is made of feathers from parrots that pass over our corrugated metal roofs every evening on their way to the volcano." Ana likes Octavio's pillow interpretation. They make her want to go out to play jump rope.

On this day, as they return from delivering the tortillas, Ana tells Octavio a newer version: "I dreamed the people in the settlement were outside their homes as usual, seated along the border of the street. Far off on the dusty road beside a dust funnel the wind has stirred up, I see us returning home with empty baskets in our hands. Behind us, more people are walking, including Esteban, your father, whose hat, maybe a new hat, is easily recognizable. We all walk fast, as though something strange and awful is pursuing all of us. My mamá, Eva, your mamá Maria, and other people stand up to see us better. They sense something is wrong, so they run to join us. The whole group joins up, as Esteban and the others catch up to us. We run to arrive home. We turn to see the big machines with scissors chasing us, screaming at us. Behind them we see real tractors overtake our space. Neighbors now lie down in a horizontal line and I hear people yelling, 'Now there will be other work. Demolish the coffee groves.' Esteban and Maria stand up together to interpret the meaning of the shouting. 'They say we will lose our homes' We all stand up and look each other in the eyes and whisper, 'They will build big houses, and we will serve them and their owners.' The community we know from childhood has changed by the next day. The coffee plantations with their many trees are demolished. The community's road has been narrowed. I scream as loud as a thousand parrots. 'I say we must unite or we'll lose our community.' My words echo throughout the settlement and life goes on one more day. I see everyone hiding in holes like rats. The last thing I see are beautiful new cars filled with people dressed in nice clothes spilling out their windows, passing through our small crowd, moving their mouths and waving goodbye to us."

Ana and Octavio arrive home at the very moment she finishes telling Octavio her dream. Octavio goes into his cardboard house without saying anything more to Ana. Ana quietly returns to her home. Life is still as poor as always inside the cardboard houses, lit within by candlelight. As Octavio goes to sleep that night, his mind still trapped inside Ana's dream, he hopes her nightmare dream will come true for these people inside their cardboard houses.

...after...CAROLINA RIVERA ESCAMILLA

When The Poinsettias Were White

When I was in fourth grade, I learned in my social studies class that the Spanish founded El Salvador. "Pedro de Alvarado," said the teacher, "was the great conquistador who led the Spanish to civilize the Indians of Cuzcatlán." The phrase "the Spanish civilized the Indians" jumps into my memory like a frog into mud, and called to mind my youngest brother's godmother. She was from Spain, (and we were very proud of him because he was the only one who had a godmother different from the rest of the us.) Mamá calls her "la Españolita, la señorita fina," because of her fragile complexion.

"La Españolita," Mamá used to say, "is a good and beautiful person. She has given construction work to your dad." Papá used to fix things at her house.

As I walked home from school, I wondered why we did not look like la Españolita with her fine beautiful fair skin. I wanted to know whether my grandparents or great-grandparents were from Spain, and whether they spoke like la Españolita.

I arrived home at almost one o'clock. Mamá was standing at the wood-burning stove, feeding pieces of wood into it, causing the pomegranate-colored embers to flame into a hotter fire. As she peeled layers off a small white onion, I said, "Good afternoon, Mamá." She turned around, looking heavy and tired. She was pregnant.

"Good afternoon, daughter, where are your sister and brothers?" She continued cooking. I had forgotten all about my sister and brothers, but realized they would come soon. I came closer to the stove and pushed the embers with my yellow pencil. "Stop! You will burn yourself."

"Mamá, where do we come from? Where did my grandparents and great-grandparents come from? Why don't we look like the Españolita?"

"Little girl, where have you come up with all those questions? Chop this onion for the rice." She handed me a small pale onion.

"I don't want to cook. I want to know where we come from."
Mamá took the onion and chopped it up, then threw into the pan
as the lard melted. "I am busy right now," Mamá said.

"The teacher said today that a man named Pedro de Alvarado
led the Spaniards to civilize the Indians from Cuzcatlán. Am I
civilized? Are we Indians, Mamá? Why don't we look like la
Españolita?"

"Daughter, I do not have time to answer your questions right
now. I have to go to drop off lunch to your dad at work. When I
come back this evening, I will tell you a story that your grandma
told me about the Indians."

Evening came, and as she promised, Mamá told the story
seated by the light of several skinny ten-cent candles melted
directly to the surface of the big rectangular red Formica table la
Españolita had sold her in several payments. She sipped from her
cup of hot chocolate, as she kept an eye on my brothers at play
on the floor.

"Before the Spanish came, our people spoke only Nahuat. The
poinsettias in the whole country were white. Indians used to
gather and celebrate the birth of new poinsettias."

"Why are they red now, Mamá?"

"The Spaniards killed so many Indians their blood turned the
poinsettias red."

"Why did the Spanish kill the Indians?"

"Not all of them, since you are my little Indians. There are
many out there who do not want to be Indians, and neither do
they want to be called such." As Mamá finished the story, she
blew out the candles. My brothers and sister were already
nesting like kittens in their bed.

The Españolita used to visit us almost every Sunday. She
brought us packages of Diana cookies, blond in color, soft and
milky in the middle, layered cookies, nothing special. I think
Mamá felt a little pressured to ask her to be my baby brother's
godmother. It is the biggest honor you can give someone, as the
godparent becomes your family. Mamá had a lot of children to
give as goddaughters or godsons.

One Sunday when the Españolita was coming to visit us, my sister, brothers, and I prepared spears, and slingshots, like the Apache Indians we have seen on TV in the evenings in the house of El Chele, my littler brother's friend, as we do not have a TV. I have also seen pictures of Indians in my older brothers' history books. We even plucked several feathers from the hens to put them on our heads, like the picture in the book. We painted our faces with soot from the ashes under the *comal* on the stove.

When la Españolita arrived at the door, we surrounded her, chanting songs like the Apache Indians, and brandishing our weapons. My brother shot her and got her on her delicately long giraffe neck with his slingshot. She screamed for help.

"Girls, boys, stop! What is wrong with all of you?" Mamá came running out of the kitchen with a stick in her hand. "Sorry *comadre*, ah, these children are playing at being Indians today."

The godmother sat down on the first chair she saw, rubbing her neck with her right hand. Mamá took me by the hand and swatted me with the stick on my legs.

"Dalia! You are the inventor of this problem. Your brothers and sister could have killed her with those slingshots." She whacked me one more time on my legs; it stung like habana chiles in the mouth.

I pursed my lips and, pulled out the hen's feather from my hair, and softly told Mamá, "But she and her people killed the Indians from Cuzcatlán, from here, Mamá." "Daughter, that happened more than five-hundred years ago, and she was not the one who killed them."

I felt like our dog Sultan, hiding his tail, and bending his head low when he is caught eating food that does not belong to him. I stayed in my bed all day wondering whether the Españolita would ever bring us cookies again.

…after…CAROLINA RIVERA ESCAMILLA

Teresa/ La Siguanaba

Teresa always manages to make ends meet in very creative ways. She knits aprons or tablecloths. She cleans rich people's houses, where she likes to read the copies of *Life Magazine* she picks out of the trash. She serves as a waitress sometimes in family restaurants. She works at the circus: cleaning, doing laundry, and cooking for the performers. Mostly she likes cutting coffee from their branches, handpicking and stripping the slimy red fruit that holds the coffee beans. She is careful to pick only red and never the yellow or green fruit. She tries not to injure any branches, especially when the caporales are watching the workers. She enjoys flirting with the guys. She and her son Dennis have come to live with us again. They are staying in the unfinished mansion, sharing space in the unfinished basement with our Tía Yita. Just like her husbands, jobs never last long with Teresa. In my heart, she is my favorite cousin, even though my Tía Yita says that Teresa is cursed by La Siguanaba. By that, Tía Yita means that Teresa is a loose woman.

Today, Teresa invites my sister and me to walk with her on the path we used to take to elementary school. She opens the curtain that separates our room from the living room and says, "Let's go find a job in the coffee groves." She breezes in and settles on the edge of our wooden bed like a dropping leaf whose wind is cut off by the curtain as it closes. She holds a small basket, ready to work. Her apron has big pockets and wraps around her. Her full face, the color of copper pennies, wears a big smile.

"Let's go then," we say, already dressed in jeans and kicker shoes with tire-tread soles. My sister is wearing John Lennon sunglasses. As we leave, I hear the wind blowing hard, then I see the first branch of the fruit-laden mango trees that has fallen in the yard. There are a scattering of baby birds and eggs on the ground. Some are still in the nest, some are next to them. We hope the mamá birds will find their babies again, so Teresa shows us how to scoop up the birds and the eggs without touching them. We put them at the bottoms of a tree trunk.

104

"And where do you think you are going?" Mamá calls from her bedroom. My parents' room, which is closest to the front door, is also divided off by flower-print polyurethane curtains stitched by the same seamstress who makes Mamá's dresses. Mamá stands in the front doorway. "We are going to find a job in the coffee groves with Teresa." I kneel down to tie my shoelaces.

"Hmm...you have no experience harvesting coffee," Mamá says to my sister and me, but I know she is addressing me. Estela and especially Teresa know what it is to pick coffee. "Besides, they only allow children with an older adult, so they can exploit both. Teresa is only nineteen, and she only looks a little older than you girls." Mamá wears a look that only mothers understand.

"Tía, we are going to be nearby, at Zelaya's Grove, where Tía Victoria and Tía Angela are working. We'll come right back if they do not take us." Teresa's childlike voice and the smile she gives Mamá make it seem as though they are only playing *pispiriraña*, the guessing game, where you put your hands behind you, hide something in one hand—as though Mamá is going to guess which hand holds the truth. No matter that Teresa already has children—Mamá still does not see Teresa as an adult.

"I want these girls here by noon, if they do not take you into the coffee grove, and I will know, because I will see Victoria." Mamá sounds like a sergeant. My Aunt Victoria is Mamá's older sister. She then examines us from toe to head. "Take off your sunglasses. You are going to work, right, or are you going to the beach?"

"My eyes get dust in them when the wind blows hard. Listen to the wind out here; it's like a hurricane." Estela, my eldest sister, says this without taking off her sunglasses. Teresa laughs a little too hard at my sister's answer to sergeant Mamá. Our Tía Yita comes from the adobe kitchen on the side of the house, where she is cooking corn and red beans in two baked clay pots to see what's going on.

Tía Yita is a genius at making a wind-blocking wall for the kitchen fire. She protects the fire from being blown out by the wind with pieces of old metal she finds in the construction debris. She also has hearing like a dog; she can hear what is going on under the earth. As she nurtures her fire, she hums a song like a mountain dove, a song from the 1950s that I have heard playing on the radios. "What's the name of the song, Auntie?" "Umm-Umm- 'Her' by Jorge Negrete," she answers staring at me, an uncertain expression on her face. From her I learn to touch flames with my index and thumb fingers without getting burned.

"Just don't fly away with La Siguanaba or get lost with her." Tía Yita says from the corner of the house, throwing a look to Mamá. Teresa, in turn, throws a look toward our Tía Yita. It's the expression of an angry child whose toy someone has taken away.

Tía Yita's mention of La Siguanaba has almost always been connected to Teresa, even when we were much smaller. Teresa, my sister, and I often walked through the coffee groves. During the Christmas of 1970, Teresa, Estela, and my brothers and I went to cut coffee berries to make a pretend Christmas tree. We would often play hide and seek at the coffee groves close to home. And since we never had a real Christmas tree we used the pretend one until the leaves became brownish like the old photos of mamá's grandmother, and our great-grandmother.

Now I like the way Teresa answers Tía Yita, because she was so emotional and always ready to fight when we were little. Tía Yita's words have always been as startling as the end-of-recess bell, just when we're enjoying a game. When we were little, Teresa would laugh at our aunt and say things like, "Why do you always make me out to be a monster, señora?" Teresa's words sounded serious, and were usually accompanied by her standing with her hands on her hips, ready for a fight. When Teresa spoke to Tía Yita, everyone in the house would tense up, especially Teresa's mother, Aunt Lina. Ordinarily, Aunt Lina is known for her patience and having a heart as calm as a still lake.

Aunt Lina knows that if Tía Yita and Teresa fight, they will both start throwing things. They launch whatever is near them: sticks, knives, fire, rocks, pots, pans, hammers, brooms, shovels—it is a dangerous battlefield. Now that Teresa is a mother she sees the world differently. Today she just says, "Tía Yita, La Siguanaba never cursed me, and she never killed anyone. It is the National Guard who has been killing, raping, and making innocent women and men crazy all this time. Let's not blame each other for their crimes." Tía Yita is as surprised as we are by Teresa's words. Instead of getting defensive, Tía Yita just walks away and returns to the stove.

I take my cousin's hand and my sister's, too, as we run up the five stairs to the street. From higher up the street I look back to see my Tía Yita watching us from outside the house. I wave just before we lose sight of her, just as we exit the street to go on the path that passes our old school and takes us to the coffee groves.

Estela and Teresa walk ahead of me for the first third of a mile. I run to catch up to them, but I like to slow down to look into the shadowy gaps among the big eucalyptus and walnut trees at the edge of the coffee groves. Today, the sun and the wind create many shades of light. Just inside the coffee groves, I watch the sunlight as it filters through gaps full of wind-whipped coffee trees and other tall, swaying trees. For a moment, I imagine the shadows on the dusty and leafy ground to be invisible children hop-scotching or swimming. But something undreamed moves quickly among the walnut and eucalyptus trees. Whatever it is, it throws its shadow as it flits from behind a tree. Then, it runs to hide behind yet another tree. As I get deeper between the gaps that separate the coffee trees, I duck down so the shadow thinks I am gone. I see the shadow move again, and I think I see footprints that only a human can leave. A dry branch snaps and falls. As I run back to the path to catch up to Teresa and Estela, I run into Teresa, with my sister just behind her.

" Let's go. Run," I scream. The three of us flee down the path bordered by mixed coffee groves and big trees.

"What did you see?" Teresa asks.

"The naked man—run, run," I say.

"Or maybe it's La Siguanaba," Estela says.

"No, it's the naked man. The footprints were the shadows of a rapist."

"How do you know?" Teresa asks.

"Because they look like the same footsteps they found when Mercedes was raped and killed." I say.

107

We run about a mile until we stop as we see Calistro, the man who pastures his cows all around the area. Everyone in the *colonia* knows him. Although we greet him, we do not trust him, because people say he is in love with one of his cows and sleeps with her. They say, if someone touches or stares at the cow he's in love with, he'll start chasing you with sticks and throwing rocks. People say he is a madman. Poor Calistro—he walks behind his three big cows with a stick and a looped lasso under his left arm. We say hello to him but when he sees us, he only lifts his chin as a sign of greeting.

I want to tell him we saw the naked man, but Teresa stops me, saying, "Maybe he's the naked man." The cow's eyes look big and sad, as if embarrassed about something. The cow has smooth light brown skin. Is she the one he loves? We pass them, and I turn around to look at sun-baked Calistro walking with his head raised up as though he is praying for something. Maybe he prays for the cow he loves to become human. I imagine him cuddling with the big cow with the saddest eyes, giving her kisses. I laugh at such silliness.

"Come on, don't get so far behind." Estela complains. "Why are you laughing, girl? You're just scared. I think you saw a shadow, not the naked man."

"No, it was the naked man." I say as though I'm sure. I struggle to understand the idea that a man, maybe this man, raped my friend Mercedes and killed her as she tried to run away from him. Mamá says that there is not just one such man; that there are many men around the *cafetales* waiting for a girl or a woman walking alone to rape and then to kill.

"Do not ever walk by yourself around the cafetales, and always carry a stick in your hand as you pass them," Mamá instructs my sisters and even my brothers.

"Never walk by yourself on this path. Other women and I have encountered the naked man. One day we almost killed him with a machete." Teresa says this, as she picks up a sharpened stick.

" I know." Estela nods in agreement with her, and says to me, "You could easily be attacked because you're such a dreamer."

"You are always distracted. You're too curious. You could have been taken away back there, if we hadn't stopped to come look for you. Maybe you were just imagining things there. And what were you doing? Were you looking for dirt to eat?" Now Teresa sounds like my mother, and then she laughs. Her eyes remind me of the cows' eyes—big, sad and black.

" I don't eat dirt anymore. Besides, I only did that when I was little," I say. "I learned that from Eva when she used to take care of me."

"Yes, and you almost died from parasites, because you were eating dirt from the cemetery," Estela says, sounding like a resentful child.

Teresa laughs a laugh that sounds like a flock of wild squawking parrots taking off. This time she throws a tender look at me. I know they are making fun of me for not walking as fast as they do.

The wind makes trees sway and sketches lively shadows on the path. It smells like guavas, oranges, and ripe bananas. It's still very windy and from behind, I giggle as my sister's and my cousin's hair flies upward. "It is better for you to walk next to us, if you do not want what happened to your little friend Mercedes to happen to you," Teresa says. I think about Mercedes, who would have been fourteen like me Or maybe she was a year older than me. We were in fifth grade when she died. When the wind picks up the dust, the green from the coffee grove looks darker.

When Teresa and Estela get to the path we used to take to go to school when we were smaller, they stop under a walnut tree and wait for me to join them.

"Do you remember when we picked up the nuts and smashed them with a rock to find the meat?" Teresa asks. She picks up some dried up nuts that the wind has knocked from the almost-dead tree. When I was in second grade, this tree stood in the middle of a thick jungle and was full of walnuts "The forest is being amputated by criminals," Papá says. Sometimes it's dangerous to be around here now, because it has become the dumping place for the military to leave dead bodies of the *muchachos,* meaning *guerrilleros.* My cousin leans against the trunk of the tree with a walnut in her hand, trying to press it open.

109

"I remember, that was the day you stopped coming to school," Estela says looking up. She reaches for something in the crotch of a branch and the tree trunk. I look up and see swaying branches and strips of a blue sky in between. Teresa turns quiet. We all sit down on the ground and I lie down under the tree, looking up. Teresa and Estela follow my example.

"I stopped coming because Mamá married that evangelical man and we moved away from you," Teresa says. "Then I met the evangelical boy who used to wait for me in the middle of the road going to school, and that's why Tía Yita says La Siguanaba touched me." She laughs.

Remember that Tía Yita also accused our cousin Octavio of being touched by la Siguanaba because he acts like a girl. I say this and an image of my cousin comes to me. I see him in girls's clothes playing to be teacher Julita. It was just a game.

When I was little Tía Yita told me, "La Siguanaba bewitched your cousin Teresa when she was playing in the coffee grove, and turned her into a monster woman. Don't go by yourself to play in the grove. That ugly woman will touch you and turn you into another monster woman and no man will ever want you after that."

In my mind, I can still see those moonlit evenings when we sat in front of our house, watching the forest and listening to Tía Yita talk about La Siguanaba. I would admit that I was then afraid of this woman, but at the same time I wanted to be like her, La Siguanaba, she has powers.

Teresa, a few years older than Estela and me, protested the accusations Tía Yita heaped on her, but Tía Yita never listened.

Then and now, I prefer Teresa's version of the story. She says La Siguanaba kills men by taking the form of a beautiful submissive woman to attract them to her. Once alone with them, she uses her long, sharp fingernails to stab them in their eyes and smashes their heads with a rock until they die. Other men disappear, it is said, because she keeps them in a cave. La Siguanaba goes to the canyon in Sol Millet, where a creek flows to wash her long, floppy tits. She slaps her tits against the rocks like laundry, and cries for her son El Cipitillo who was stolen from her. I am sure Teresa has heard this story of La Siguanaba from other women too. After all, it is a mythical character.

"Does she hate women?" I ask.

"If you have children, she might try to steal them from you, but she does not hate women. If you are a young girl, she bewitches you, and you will be like her," my cousin Teresa laughs.

The wildness of the wind and the flapping walnut leaves makes me wonder whether the mystery of La Siguanaba ever touched my cousin Teresa. Or does just thinking of the myth of this monster woman dancing in the dusty wind that swoops over us three girls simply add to the mystery of La Siguanaba? My Tía Yita's talking about her, and the fact that all my other Aunts, great-grandmothers, grandmothers, with the exception of my Mamá, were all abandoned by the fathers of their children. Some of their children died early, or at least very young. Or is she talking about Aunt Queta, who left her child crying too long in the hammock, even after Grandma reminded her to go attend to him?

Aunt Queta said she thought the baby would develop stronger lungs and adjust better to this world if she didn't attend to him the moment he started crying. Aunt Queta was nineteen at the time. She was doing the father's and child's laundry, when, the sudden silence of the baby followed a long wave of his wailing. The child had strangled itself among the hammock strings. Grandma and the child's father said Queta was cursed by La Siguanaba. They forced Aunt Queta to drink and bathe in a special herbal mixture made by Grandma. It prevented Aunt Queta from ever becoming pregnant again. They were hoping this would prevent her from becoming a crazy woman, like La Siguanaba, who wanders the canyons creeks looking for her dead child. After the drink and bath, Aunt Queta slept a month. One day she finally got up, went to work and adopted Eva, the child of a friend who passed away from tuberculosis.

111

Teresa stands up, sighs, and sits down next to me, still under the walnut tree. The wind is soft and sounds as if it might just go to sleep. "What are you inventing in your mind?" she mutters.

"Were you ever touched by La Siguanaba, like Tía Yita says?" I ask.

"That señora is crazy. She is my Aunt, but I think she hates me because I know something about her that Mamá told me that I am not supposed to tell." Teresa looks up into the clean blue sky.

"What it is?" I sit up straight.

"Leave Tía Yita alone!" Estela barks like our dog Capullo, who is small, but with a thunderous bark.

"Did you ever meet La Siguanaba?" I ask trying to obey Estela's command.

"Yes, I even had lunch with her in the Sol Millet's canyon. We rode the bicycle together looking for el Cipitillo." She laughs, leans back, and reaches to snap off a dry branch from the walnut tree. She breaks it in pieces and makes a triangular pyramid shape on the flat clean piece of ground before her. "Here, look, maybe La Siguanaba will come cook for us." She laughs again, but her laugh fades into an angry hurt sound.

"Are you writing a book or something? Why are you asking her about La Siguanaba?" Estela sounds like an angry teacher. The wind rallies to blow a bit harder. Estela's light brown hair has been blown all over her face. She stands up and tries to smooth it down.

"There, you see, she is La Siguanaba!" Teresa says, pointing to Estela's hair-covered face.

"Every time Teresa is here, she has just left some man with her children. She's been with different men and has four children already." I say as I walk around the chubby, big-boned tree. Once it was a majestic tree with lots of walnuts. Teresa changes the subject. "Your hair is growing. I am going to braid your hair. Always use *Zapuyulo* shampoo so that it will grow strong." She always carries pieces of string, and red, yellow, green beads in her bag to decorate hair. I find it amazing that she has brought these beads with her on this walk, but she gets frustrated with my hair, because it is too coarse and straight to hold her beadwork.

"What happened to Hernán?" I ask as her hands move through my hair.

She says, "One day you'll be with a man, and if he or his family lay a finger on you, leave him and leave the children with him, but name the infant first." I say, "I thought Hernán was a nice guy. He looks like a nice guy." I play with the beads in my hands. Teresa says, "You think so? He was a nice man, but I didn't want him always at my side, and he's gone from my life." She explodes with a big laugh my Tía Yita would find very suspicious. If Tía Yita were here with us, she would look up into the sky to pray for Teresa."Come on, we are supposed to go find work." Estela gets up abruptly, as though she has just broken out of a trance.

We leave the walnut tree. Walking through the loud wind that has picked up again, I'm thinking about the only child Teresa ever keeps with her, the sweet round-faced Dennis. She never leaves Dennis with any of the men she's been with, but she has often left Dennis with us. We take care of him like one of our little brothers. When she comes back a week or so later after working somewhere, she brings each of us girls a nice blouse, and gives us some money. Then she takes off somewhere else with Dennis at her side. I don't think my cousin Teresa was touched by La Siguanaba, no matter what my Tía Yita says. Teresa loves men in her own way. Her way is to get pregnant by each man, and then to leave him with their child after she gives birth, especially when they are daughters. She seems to want to prove something, but I do not know what.

The last time Teresa visited, I was finishing middle school and she had come in search of a name for her new baby girl. For whatever reason, my cousin entrusts us with the task of naming her children, before she leaves them with the father. She knows that we don't like names from soap operas, unlike most young mothers these days. Teresa comes into Mamá and Papá's bedroom and lifts her blouse, and from her pants' waist she pulls out a paper she has pleated into a fan. She spreads it open, fans herself, and then starts reading the names. There are ten names she copied from magazines she gets from the circus. Most of the names are from Mexican soap operas or are of actresses from the USA. "Let me see your list," Mamá says. My sister and I sit on the edge of the big wooden bed on either side of Mamá. Then the three of us read the list aloud.

"Mamá, why do you put powder on your face?" Estela has been observing Mamá since we came in at the bedroom, where Mamá has been combing her long brown hair, and applies some pinkish Maja powder to her cheeks and forehead.

"It shoos away the mosquitoes," Mamá answers, smoothing some hair back from her face.

"Then put some on me." Estela takes the rounded powder box from Mamá's bag. Mamá pats Estela's tiny thin silky face with the powdering sponge. With powder on her face, Estela stands up straight and plays the coquette, somehow feeling older than she did a moment ago. The powder smells like a mix of roses and baby powder.

I read the names aloud one more time: Cristal, Isela, Jane, Joanna, Monica, Linda, Silvia, Alison, Diana, Cristina. Mamá says, "Those names have nothing to do with family memory, although maybe just one of them does, but you would not know about her. They are from movies and soap operas, from lives that only exist on screens." Teresa sits next to me, pushes me a bit to make space on the bed for herself. She laughs and the rooster outside crows, as if answering her. Estela and I start saying names from the family, "Paula, Ana, Lorena, Petrona, Alicia, Angela, Alma, Lola, Antonia." We three girls laugh about the name 'Antonia,' because we know someone called 'La negra Antonia,' who is very big, beautiful and funny. Mamá remains on the edge of the bed.

"Stand up in front of me." Mamá looks hard at Teresa, whose eyes are closed. "How did you feel about your baby girl when she was born?"

"Happy, healthy, and loved." Teresa's voice does not match the emotions of her words; her tone sounds childish, even embarrassed. A moment later, she opens her big luminous black eyes, and she laughs.

"Then baptize her Felicia Magdalena," Mamá says getting up. Teresa likes the name. Then she tells us to start cleaning the house. She goes outside to start cooking the pot full of red beans that Tía Yita had cleaned. Teresa joins us in the housecleaning. She looks like a sunflower—erect with a very happy glow. My little brothers and sisters who were outside playing under the mango tree run inside the house looking for Mamá.

I remember the day Teresa arrived with Felicia Magdalena. I had been feeling strange all that week, repeatedly leaving the house, just to stand in the middle of the street, as though I was waiting for somebody important to come along, or *something* important to happen. My girlfriends' constant chatter about boys, menstrual periods, and kotexes left me jealous and annoyed that I still hadn't been included in that club. I was feeling like a small green mango ready to change its color to become a real ripening mango. Then there was the pain in my chest—or maybe it was in my small breasts—and my abdomen and even in my itchy vagina. I really didn't know how I could talk to anyone about these feelings. Estela is quite private, and had become quieter and angrier than when she was in middle school.

Back in the house, while still under the spell of these strange feelings, Teresa walks straight into my room and catches me with my right hand in my panties, touching my thing. The curtain is all that divides the living room from the so-called bedrooms. She stands there with the baby girl in her arms. "Who shows up unannounced at nine o'clock in the morning on a weekday!" I wonder. It's summer, the month of November---no school. You can hear the wind sweeping across the metal Duralite roof. Usually my aunt or one of my little brothers yells, "La Teresa is coming." But not this time. Quietly moving aside the bedroom curtain, she startles me.

"Uh! What are you doing? Does it itch? That means you need a man or the Red Old Man is visiting you soon." Teresa says. I take my hand out of my panties. "No, I think I have an infection. I was just checking why it's so itchy."

"If my Aunt or Uncle sees you doing that, they'll hit your butt," she says looking at me with those shiny black eyes. She puts the baby girl in the center of the bed, and goes to get Dennis whom she left outside the house. At least the little boy didn't see me with my hands in my panties.

115

I remember Teresa stopped visiting with me and my sisters for the first time when she was thirteen. I was still very young, but I tried to listen to everything the women said.

My mother says, "How far along?" joining my Aunt Lina outside our house very early in the morning. "Ay! This girl has twisted her destiny," Aunt Lina bends her head and spits on the ground, and then smears the spit into the dirt with her right shoe tip. She usually does not do that—spit on the ground. Aunt Lina is very clean. There must be something very wrong with her today. Mamá and Aunt Lina walk over to where my Tía Yita is sleeping. I follow my mother. Mamá tells Aunt Lina that I am not a child who sleeps deeply, which is true. Their quiet conversation has woken me up. Any noise, even birdsong wakes me up. "I want to go with you. Why is Aunt Lina here so early?" My mom purses her lips, which means "no," but takes me with them anyway. The three women walk fast and talk in secrets. I look at the sky and the big star on the horizon. My father says it is the star of the Three Wise Men. It is five thirty in the morning and the C-shaped moon is very high. The birds are still sleeping.

When we arrive at my Aunt Lina's house, they send me to Teresa's room. I like her house, because it is like a real house with bedrooms and a living room with real walls. The house is like a home church. Her stepfather is an evangelical pastor. The house has two wings, a tile roof, and two wood beams. Outside there is a patio with guava trees, a custard apple tree and a piece of land for flowers that is surrounded by a fabric to protect it from the chickens and dogs. They have water and two concrete vats for washing clothes. Inside it is dark, which I do not like, and the window in my cousin's room is rectangular and small with a metal grill. My aunt Lina says, "The boy used to leave roses there, and that's how they fell in love." It makes me laugh when I hear this, because I cannot imagine Teresa accepting roses from any boy. But I still like her house. It feels more organized than our house.

"One day, they," referring to the neighbors around the evangelical man's house, "are going to throw them all away like

116

old donkeys," says my father angrily when this subject comes up. "That's what they do when you are settlers for those colonist companies. "They," the Evangelic man, and Aunt Lina, "are only colonists; they do not own the land, even if they built their own houses on it. They are little better than slaves. When they do not want you anymore, they take the house away, too."

"Why aren't we colonists, too, so we can get one of those houses?" I ask him.

"I worked my way up to become an independent master builder in construction. I have never worked as a slave for those foreign companies. I have to be free. We all need to be free." He tells me this with a brave expression in his eyes but with an exhausted tone that tells me to shut up. Papá swears often at me and my brothers, saying that Mamá and he preferred being thrown out from the *caserios* settlement of Antiguo Cuscatlán rather than forcing my Grandma to hand over Mamá to German landowner and businessman, Walter Thilo Denninger. When Mamá forewarned Papá about this horrible possibility early in their courting, my Papá bought a hen and a rooster. Mamá and he looked each other in the eyes, and promised that their children would never become colonists, like Mamá's childhood friend Alfonsina and her children. "One day the colonist status has to be ended for our people," Papá says again and again.

Papá makes me regret saying I like the evangelical man's house. I've seen the tractor with a deer on it, and something about a John Deere Company printed on it, too. I do not call him Teresa's stepfather, because she does not see this man like that. Aunt Lina says that he works as a security guard. Mi Papá tells us that he married Aunt Lina because she owns a house, so he can take from her. "He's just a colonist," he tells me pointing at me with his comb, and then he combs his shiny hair with Vaseline. " But Teresa has a nice bedroom," I scream at him as I exit the house to play.

When I go into her bedroom, Teresa is lying on her wine-colored wooden bed staring at the ceiling. My mother tells me to stay close to Teresa and not to ask any questions. I would have lain down next to my cousin, except I want to hear my mother and my aunts' conversation. I walk quietly to the square bedroom window facing the garden where the women walk in silence, their lips moving in prayers, I guess. My mother has a shovel, and my Tía Yita is holding a small white cotton blanket, with something like a misshapen baby bird on it, or maybe it is more like a small overripe mango. For a moment it looks as though my aunts and Mamá are planting a tree. But the arrangements are too mysterious for planting a tree. Teresa looks at me and says, "Psst, psst, did they bury the monster yet?"

"What?" I squat quickly below the window ledge for fear of the three women catching sight of me. Teresa's eyes are now nailed to my face, but with a smile. "Did they bury the monster yet?" Teresa asks again.

"What monster?" I do not say this aloud.

"The one that came out of my...my... mouth." She says this, then moves her legs slightly and returns to staring at the ceiling. Her eyes are not normal...somehow she seems distracted. "You mean the thing that my Tía Yita has in her hands? I thought they were rotten tortillas wrapped in a napkin." I am trying to make a joke. I sit on her side of the bed and stare at her shiny, full, brown face.

"Did they finish burying the monster?" Her anger lights up the center of the bed looking at me with a bright child's face. This time I am afraid of her face's expression. Her big black eyes are lost in a place I cannot describe. "Let me see." I go to the window to spy again.

"Hey, Teresa, Aunt Lina has the shovel and she is digging a hole close to the fence, next to where the hens sleep."

"No, tell them the hens will dig it out." She says this angrily, and then she laughs quietly under the blanket.

"I can't go tell them. Mamá will beat me if she knows I know about your monster...wait, they are moving to the other side, you know, close to the guava tree. That will be a good place to bury that thing. Your monster might be good food for the tree to grow healthy guavas."

"Shh, quiet, you want to wake up my little brother!" Her tone shifts from anger to complaining from where she is hidden under blankets. I have totally forgotten about my little cousin.

"My Aunt has finished digging the hole. Mamá is taking the thing from my Tía Yita's hands. It looks like a baby bird that fell from its nest, like those we used to find on the ground in summer time, or maybe a small dead duck, or a chick wrapped in a blanket."

"I told you it's a monster and it is full of blood. It came out from my mouth." She shifts her position in bed, facing the wall opposite the window. Teresa reaches for something under her bed. It is a statue of El San Martin de Porres, the black saint.

The three women finish the job. Nobody prays after they bury the thing. I say, "Hide the saint. My aunt is coming now."

"I don't care," she says, tucking the saint under the blanket. "How did the monster, I mean that thing, appear in your mouth?"

"Because I slept with Marcos and he put the monster inside," she says sitting up.

I know Marcos. She met him when she was getting baptized to become an evangelical. She swore at everyone during the service. Her stepfather, the evangelical man, said that she needed a man to put her in her place. She was only twelve and a half. She stopped going to school. I missed her because she always stood up for my sister and me when the older girls at school hit us. Also, she played jump rope for hours, and never got tired. My sister and I would run behind when she rode the bicycle Aunt Lina bought for her. My sister and I were as happy as though we were the ones riding the bike. After Aunt Lina moved away with the evangelical man, the bike rusted in their new house.

"Marcos, that timid toad, the ugly guy who plays with you sometimes, the one who looks up in the sky and the birds shit in his mouth?" I ask.

"Yes! That one," Teresa says and breaks into a laugh. I laugh with her. I go to the window to see if the women are coming. The sun is already up. The birds are flying everywhere... and four of them are already on top of the monster's grave. "Mi mamá and Aunts are coming. Go to sleep." I jump back into Teresa's bed, and we both pretend to sleep.

Aunt Lina threw out all the saints when she married the evangelical man. Teresa doesn't care about evangelicals, or about Catholic things. She keeps the black saint to hurt my Aunt's feelings. I hear Mamá saying this whenever Aunt Lina complains about Teresa. Whenever Aunt Lina tries to discipline

my cousin, Teresa takes out the black saint and holds it in my
Aunt Lina's face. "You're going to go to hell together with your
new husband. This is my saint and you're not taking him away
from me. I believe in saints, you believe in devils like that one
who gets on top of you every night." Teresa laughs and threatens
the evangelical man, saying she will cut his throat like a hen. My
Aunt Lina ends up in her bedroom sobbing quietly while the
evangelical man and Teresa quarrel in the living room. He says,
"You have the devil inside your soul, woman." My mother says
that the evangelical man doesn't realize that Teresa is just a
young girl with hatred toward him for stealing her mother. "The
devil has possessed you." He tries to slap Teresa. Teresa throws
the heavy ceramic saint at his face and it lands between his eyes.
His nose starts to leak blood. The Saint loses his two legs in the
fight, but Teresa rescues the saint and runs away to my house.

Estela, Teresa, and I walk in silence for a few minutes. Teresa
eats the dried nuts or pretends to be eating them. Estela, still
wearing her sunglasses, is playing with the big leaf that fell on
her face. She rips the leaf slowly along its veins. We pass
through the canyon that divides our community from the Sol
Millet settlement, where Teresa's family lives. In the middle of
the canyon is a creek where La Siguanaba is believed to wash
her large tits. Every time we would visit Teresa, we run fast
through the canyon so La Siguanaba can't touch us. Teresa
laughs and says, "This is the place where I first kissed that timid
toad Marcos. I was going to school and he said he would
accompany me through the dangerous canyon. I told him he
could." Teresa asks us to sit a while to listen to the creek but we
can't hear much water. "The tractors excavated the canyon, and
buried the creek, as well as my first kiss," Teresa sighs.
    "I think it is good these tractors are filling in the canyon, so we
won't hear about any more rapes or killings, and besides I have
had so many nightmares about this canyon. I still have them
sometimes," Estela says. "I just hope I remember the scent of the
eucalyptus trees and the tractors do not destroy them all." Estela
sighs.
    I ask, " What ever happened to Marcos?"

"What?" Teresa mutters. After a moment, she says, "He's gone, swallowed up, buried, under the earth like the fetus he planted in me. He ran away once he knew I lost his baby. Why are you asking about him now?"

"It was a fetus the thing Mamá and my aunts buried at the evangelical man's house?"

"Yes, and keep in mind that it was a monster and now it is part of the earth, water, dead fruits and humans that these tractors are digging up now." She laughs again.

"But then you had Dennis. He's his son too."

"Possible...*niña*, what's with you and all these questions? she says breaking a nut.

Far away we hear voices. We get up and walk a bit and then stop on the path. The coffee pickers are going to lunch. "We need to return home, we do not have work or coffee" Estela says.

"No, let's go pick some coffee to sell, now that the pickers are at lunch," Teresa says. We hide behind an old rubber tree, then we go to the coffee grove to fill her basket with coffee berries that the pickers have put aside in sacks. Then we pick some from the tree. I put one in my mouth. It is very sweet and slimy with the pit or bean inside. I spit it out. We walk home taking turns carrying the full basket of coffee on our heads. "Let's go sell it first," Teresa says. "It's about ten pounds." Estela feels the weight of the basket on her head. "Where do we sell it?" I ask taking the basket from Estela to put it on my head. "Let's go to Don Chico's *finca*." Teresa sighs. Don Chico's *finca* is another coffee grove not far from our home, maybe two miles over hilly roads. We drink fresh water at Don Chico's every time we pass it.

Despite the strong mid-morning wind, the sun heats the crowns of our heads. I feel as though my brain is cooking. The gale has swept the dirty roads revealing smooth , bone-colored paths. I do not know what makes me think of the always neat sidewalks of cemeteries. I like the month of November, when it is dry. The blue skies, with their fat, white clouds flow continuously, like waves of foam breaking across an infinite sea. We walk home on, happy to have money in our pockets.

121

The wind makes messes with everything that is normally set and stable. A pink *Maquilishuat* flower has fallen on Teresa's head. I like it there, because it reminds me of when we would hairpin flowers to decorate our heads, when we were littler. The wind today has mostly dismembered childhood memories: recalling stories of La Siguanaba, the monster woman, remembering my aunts' comments the day my mamá and aunts buried my cousin's monster. Stirred up memories are reassembled in the present, so that I want to ask Teresa about the evangelical boy who got her pregnant. I think about sex, what it must be like, and whether she got pregnant the first time she laid down with Marcos? I also realize that her stepfather stole her mother and stole her childhood from her. I want to ask her whether that's why she fights and laughs all the time. But I don't ask. I wonder whether she will ever spend another day like this with Estela and me? I am afraid...

Mamá has a photo of Teresa when she was eight years old. In the photo, she is holding a yellow toy duck in one hand and her elementary reading book under her arm, and she is smiling. I'll show her the picture tonight, because tonight there will be a full moon, bright and clean, thanks to November's wind. I'll plant a *ruda* tree for her on the right side of the patio where the sun bathes the plants. *Ruda* leaves can cure almost anything. Mamá says people have used these fragrant leaves for centuries. We use it for Mamá when she gets seizures or attacks. She says she feels better after we put the leaves under her nostrils. She says it calms her down. I think it might bring some of childhood's happiness back to Teresa. Perhaps it will pull out all her anger and protect her from the angry spirits I have heard Amelia, Mamá's long-time friend and seamstress, mention. I run to catch up with Teresa and Estela who are far ahead of me again. We need to arrive home together.

Teresa likes the photo. She puts it back in my hands and sighs long and deep. She leaves the next day with her son. I get the *ruda* trees from Amelia. I plant three, one for Teresa, for Tía Yita, and for Aunt Lina. I know that deep inside Aunt Lina must be angry and sad for not understanding Teresa's rage. Mamá says, "Teresa will come back." Teresa returns two days later to stay with us long enough for the *ruda* trees to bloom yellow

122

flowers. By the time she tells us the news that she will join a circus going to Puerto Rico, the *ruda* tree has dried out and turned brown. Teresa is going away happy. She takes her only son with her, and sometimes she leaves her daughters for a while with Aunt Lina, but eventually all the girls are deliveries Teresa makes to their fathers. I am hoping she will return with Dennis only (not with a new child) for the following coffee harvest next November.

Lucio Molina Linares

It is Sunday. My sisters and brothers and I are playing with an old tire, letting it roll down from the little flat area where the improvised house stands, down the canyon where the tire runs out of force at the bottom of the basin. Sometimes it just stops and falls over; sometimes it turns and rolls around the trees at the bottom. My sister and brother run down to bring the tire back to the top to roll it down again.

We hear a yell from the street, "Ey, Demetrio Linares!" This was once my father's name. I look up to the roof where my father picks mangos and *Sunzas*. "Papá, there is a man with a woman looking for you. My cousin, Tula brought them here," I yell. My father stops reaching for fruit. A voice calls from the street, "Soy Lucio Molina Linares. I hope you remember me. This is Zoila my wife, the mother of my children." Lucio draws closer to the house. My father's chocolate-colored eyes reach Lucio. His mouth, his face, and then his whole body are alight with curiosity saying, "Achees, this is not possible. It has been thirty years. I told Pablo Funes to look for my brother when I knew he was going to the coffee fields, to work in the harvest at the finca near where I grew up."

"I was eleven the last time I saw you, Demetrio. You were seven when you ran away from Isabel, our grandmother," Lucio says. The children, as well as the hens, birds, cats, and dogs with their dancing tails stand around looking at these adults looking at one another. Tula leads my mother and Tía Yita out the entrance of the house. My father comes down the ladder from the roof to meet his brother. My new uncle is taller than my father by four inches. They both have bronzed skin, the color of the walls in the house of Armenia, a town known for its good brick and tiles. Lucio holds a bottle of *Muñeco* in his hand, at his side. His short wife is a limp flower. My father has crossed arms and a small curious smile. He does not show his pearly teeth.

"*Hombre*, you are my brother!" My father shakes hands with Lucio. "Rosita! I have found my brother. Do you remember how much I tried to find him in Santa Ana? My mother acknowledges with a nod and a smile. "*Hermano*! I gave your name to a person who works in the coffee harvest to ask about you. I gave my name to them to give to you, my birth name and my resurrected name. You know, there's no trace of my birth certificate, nor of our brothers' and sisters'. I searched the city halls of Santa Ana, El Congo, and there is no evidence that we were born." My father's voice alternates between childlike wonderment and a grown man's astonishment. He invites my uncle and his wife inside the house. The wife is quiet, and sits like the rocks my father places to support the trees. She smells like my father's workers liquor, *Espíritu de Caña*. Uncle Lucio's face is like a baby when he smiles.

"It would be better to say he found you," Mamá says with a skeptical smile, like a lioness noting her territory. "Look Rosita, Lucio's eyes are the same as mine, small like watermelon seeds. His nose has the same shape as mine, a cat's nose, but more pointed, the face of our father." My little brothers, Noe, Edwin, and Mauricio repeat in mockery what my father is saying from behind the entrance door, and then giggle. "Foolish boys, get out from there," my mother commands. "Let them be. They are happy they have a new uncle," my father says. My little brothers come out one by one to stand in front of our new uncle and his wife. My brother Javier comes from nowhere inside the little house kicking a soccer ball. He asks my new uncle to kick the ball. My uncle kicks it. Estela, my older sister, and I are sent to buy Cola Champán, and one bottle of coca cola to celebrate.

"And who are those poor strangers?" Nata the storeowner asks. "It's my uncle and his wife, and the woman with the limp is my cousin Tula." I say.

"They look so poor, so badly dressed. Where do they come from?" Nata mutters.

"They're just tired. They came from Santa Ana. They've been looking for my father all morning. My father has not seen his brother since… ay!" Estela pinches my arm.

"Don't tell this gossip everything about our uncle," Estela hisses.

"What were you saying about your uncle?" Nata gives us the sodas. "Nothing, we have to go." Estela asks to have the sodas put on credit.

125

"More strangers to the *colonia*," Nata sighs.

When my uncle Lucio starts out on this day looking for Demetrio Molina Linares, he has no luck until he stops at a chalet to buy an H*orchata*. His wife, Zoila, is dragging behind him, tired from the day's bus ride from Santa Ana to San Salvador, then from there on to Antiguo Cuscatlán. On this hot day the plastic yellow cupful of beige-colored drink they bought calms their thirst. Hope is fading in Lucio's eyes. They sit on an oak bench gazing into the blue tropical sky. He sighs and sips his drink.

"I believe in miracles. I have to find my brother." Lucio says looking at the colonial church of the pueblo.

"You are looking for your brother? What's his name?" asks a very old, extremely thin woman with long silver hair. She contemplates Lucio's face from the chalet.

"Demetrio Linares. He came here in 1949 and married a queen, a beautiful girl named Rosa." He says like he's praying.

Rumors had filtered their way back to my great-grandmother, Isabel. She had apparently followed my Dad's path through life, but was never interested in rescuing him. The thin old lady with long silver hair calls over to a man named Sebastián. "Do you know Rosa Escamilla?" A forty-year-old man comes over to join them. "He's looking for Rosita's husband, Antonio." Lucio looks confused.

"Antonio? You resemble Antonio Rivera." Sebastián smiles,

"But my brother's name is Demetrio Linares from San Isidro, from the family Linares Molina."

"Antonio changed his name. He said he chose to forget his grandmother's family. He is very fond of a man named Rivera who helped him when he was a little boy. He is happy he changed his last name because he doesn't want anyone to think he is related to that *hijo de puta* president of our country, Arturo Molina."

"Do you know where he is now?"

"Well, he moved a while ago from this town. Paula, his mother-in–law, lost her tenant's house when she lost her job working on the coffee harvest *finca*. She got very sick from arthritis. She spent years in bed. Antonio was the only source economically for the family. He was having a hard time holding onto construction work. Rosita has a brother who lives up here on the Navas avenue. Antonio and he don't get along... they never did. It's like putting oil and water together. Joaquin is his name. He used to be the judge in this village in the 1940s, and he's quite conservative, very much *derechista*... opposite of Antonio. We can go up there to ask where Rosita lives now." Sebastián wipes his forehead with his hand.

My Uncle Lucio swings the burlap bag slung over his shoulder and pulls out five light green ears of corn and hands them to Sebastián. "*Gracias*, no. Don't bother to give us these *elotes*. I am sure you brought them for Antonio... he'll need it, because by now he has more children than the last time we saw him." Sebastián passes the corn back to Zoila, but Lucio insists, "I have enough, and I have been carrying the bag from far away. I need some rest, and it will be less for me to carry." Lucio stands to take the *elotes* from Zoila to give them back to Sebastián. Sebastián looks up into the face of Lucio, who is a full head taller than he. "*Hombre*, you do look like Antonio, I mean Demetrio. The warmth of his smile causes Lucio to smile from ear to ear, like the clowns' mouth painted on his face . "I have found my brother." Uncle Lucio says with a long sigh.

Estela and I set up the Formica table covering it with a plastic table cloth full of bright sunflowers and green leaves that Mamá only takes out for special occasions. Papá takes Uncle Lucio and Zoila to show the land where he will build the dream mansion. Papá walks with the blueprint drawing of the mansion under his left arm, then stops and unfolds the blueprint pointing like an engineer where the foundation would go. Our uncle and Zoila seem already worn out and confused. Papá continues talking, almost screaming at this point, very excited, lifting his arm in the air. " The mansion is going to be here, and you will be living with us too," he says putting his arm on my uncle's right shoulder.

"Your Uncle Lucio is quiet and an observer of nature, of his words, and a good listener," Mamá comments. Uncle tells Papá, " Hermano, you are a good man. You have learned on your own these technical things that I would have never learned in my life.

Our grandma, Isabel, would be proud of you if she knew what you have made of yourself" There is a silence between them.

On the table uncle Lucio and Zoila sit like brother and sister next to each other and behave like children behave in their first day of school. Papá gives a lot of food to both of them. " Eat, eat all you want. We have to eat when there is food. In that way, if famine comes around as usually it comes, we are well fed to survive and struggle for another good day."

"Thanks, *hermanito*," Uncle says, and gets up, walks to where Mamá is, and kisses her forehead. Then he kneels and says, "You are quite a beautiful woman, a virgin like they described you. Thanks for keeping my brother well." From every corner where we are sitting in the small space of the living room, we look and listen to our uncle's words; not man has ever done this kind of thing to Mamá. He returns to his seat and Papá laughs. We follow his laughter and even our dogs start barking. "The dogs are laughing, too," Zoila says, pointing to the dogs.

"We're all happy that you are with us and that Lucio and Antonio or Demetrio have found each other," Mamá says serving more Indian hen's soup to our Uncle and Aunt. The following weekend Uncle Lucio and Aunt Zoila bring their eight children. We are happy with our new cousins. The two older ones stay with us, living at home and working with Papá. Uncle Lucio's family and ours, from that day on, we always stay together.

...after...CAROLINA RIVERA ESCAMILLA

The Hug

"People say that the light of the moon is good for your eyes. It refreshes your visual energy." My father is standing next to me. I gaze at the large white moon, that hours ago was enormously red-orange as it emerged from the horizon. "I thought that the moonlight shines love, as in some poems I've read." Father walks to the other end of the terrace where he disappears into the shadow of trees. He waters the trees mornings and nights and whistles a song, "*El cafetalito,*" the same song he sings when he tells us about how he loves fishing.

Now, I look to my left, and there he is, sitting on the boulder he and my brothers brought up to the terrace with great effort from the garden below. They placed it on the side where the mico mango tree hangs close to the house. They stretched a rope as taut as they could from tree to boulder to help the tree grow straight, to straighten its bend. "We have to take care of it. It is special because, although its mangos are small, they are the sweetest." That was four years ago, and it still hasn't produced fruit. It needs water, I guess. And me? Hell knows what I need to grow some more inches. Maybe if my father cared about me as much as he does for these trees, I could have grown some more inches to be at least a meter and sixty-two centimeters.

I do not say this aloud because I know my father would defend himself by saying, "You're part of the Earth, this tree has the same right of being loved as you do. And what do you mean when you say we do not care about you?" by we, he means Mamá and him. "You're alive; you are breathing. Besides if you want to be tall I'll make some stilts for you, so you can look tall. Foolish girl! Tall women are ugly. Men like small women. You're smart. Besides, all the women from your mom's side and my family are small but strong, and that's what matters." How many times have I heard this? When I invite my friends home, we sometimes end up measuring our height with them, and they are almost always taller than me. I glance at my father for a second, as he submerges his thoughts deeply into the night horizon. He stands at the edge of the terrace. He's been caught up by the moon, which feels as though it occupies the whole universe with its light.

I feel guilty that he lost his job recently, as he has always worked, and when I say work, I mean he has been building anything that can be built. He destroys built things at home to rebuild them again. His hands are made to build houses, schools, gas stations, or walls. He's married to cement, to earth, to nails, to leveling lines and measuring tapes, and to hammers. On the other hand, he builds like a primitive in his own house. He does not believe in or want to build a bathroom for us with an indoor toilet, in a proper way like in some of my friends' homes. He had the money and the skills to do that on our land, too; but no, he believes we should be constantly in contact with the naked universe or the earth like savages, taking a bath under a mango tree with rainwater. He wants us to walk on the wet naked dirt with our feet. He wants us to feel it, to shake the trees after a rain. "Open your mouths and taste the flavor of the drops falling. Walk on the unpaved roads to villages." Why?---because in his youth he used to walk on them instead of on the new roads. Once in a while he would take a bath, jumping naked into a lake, the sea, or rivers. "If you carry worms from the earth in your hands in winter time, this means rains will still come in August. Drink water from the sea to cure yourself from any disease physical or emotional." However, Mamá tells him, "They are not children anymore. These girls need privacy." "Well, they can go behind a tree if they are so ashamed of growing up," he would laugh. Whenever mi papa would see me taking my bath outside the house under the Sunza tree, I would be wearing a long shirt to hide my breasts, and he would make comments. "Look Rosita, our little girl has your body, *pantorrillas de botellas, rellenitas.*" I would have to dunk the entire bucket into the barrel full of fresh rainwater and pour it over my body to deafen my ears from what he would be saying. It never worked, though. I would still hear Mamá agreeing, "Well, she is like me, growing a nice waist, ample breasts, an hour-glass shape and strong legs." My father loves my mother's shapely legs. Such strong legs remind him of the Italianate balustrade with its vertical columns fully formed and feminine, more like fully rounded calves than spindles. "You

131

see, we can appreciate their growing like the trees we plant. If we create walls for them to hide within, how then can we know they are changing?" Mamá disagrees with this type of macho commentary. "They are growing, and they need privacy." Mamá would then stand between his gaze and me. My father is crazy, and I often do not like him. I look up to the sky and pray in silence, "Please, God, don't make me like my mother or my grandmothers, not even my aunts. Don't give me full hips. I don't want to be pregnant all the time." One yellowish-green leaf falls from the *Sunza* tree and floats onto the barrel of water. I launch a mean glance at it, and it blows away.

Papá and I, we like to talk though. From the terrace we hear a far-off explosion that I fear has shattered a piece of the sky. "Where do you think that's happening?" Father asks drawing close to my left side. "Do you think the military are attacking again in *el Cerro de Guazapa*?" I look in the direction of those mountains. "Maybe, probably," Papá responds. The breeze is warm, and has disheveled Father's hair. He takes out his black plastic comb and rakes his hair back in place. Unlike him, I enjoy the feel of breeze in my hair, its silky texture over my face. I just let it be, wild and disorganized. The expectant silver moon floats unimpressed in the immense ocean of night. "These breezes smell antique. They don't change. They carry the same scent as the ones of 1932," Father continues combing his wavy hair back, then slips the comb into his rear pants pocket. "Dad, do you remember the massacre? What was the name of the president... the one who is responsible for all those deaths of 1932?" I shift to a more comfortable position on the cement floor of the terrace in front of him, ready to listen to his story. "Martínez!" he says with a sigh. "A monster... he killed so many innocent people. His hatred was especially indecent with the ones who called themselves communists. He called them all, everyone he killed, communists. I was a little boy." He indicates his child's height with his right hand fingers pointing just so high above his waist, and then he crosses his arms to continue. "I remember very well when my Papá hid us in holes where they would usually put the sacks of coffee in the *cafetales*, and covered us with all the dry leaves, so that when the soldiers were rounding people up from their homes and killing them, we were safe inside the earth. We never made noise, until Papá gave us a signal that they were gone. A lot of people hid like us." Fear is the thought that comes to my mind like a big black bat that swoops at too close to my mind's boundary. I excavate the holes in the *cafetales*, and imagine my grandfather hiding my father. Maybe my grandfather was like my father, something of an idealistic dreamer.

"Ah! Mi hija, when Martínez sent the soldiers to impose order on all the pueblos, hundreds, thousands of peasants were killed. They would leave the tortured bodies on the road or hang them from trees or buildings. On the road there were slaughtered children, men, women, some of them pregnant with their fetuses cut out. No, no, *hija*, that man was a devil, a monster with hatred for the poor." My father uses the same vivid tone he used the first time he told me about Martínez and the *matanza,* the slaughter. "My mother died giving birth one night while the soldiers slaughtered pregnant women. Martínez ordered soldiers to kill them, because he said their babies would just grow up to become new communists, and they needed to be exterminated before they were born. I was five years old when my Mamá Hortensia died. She was only thirty-three, my Papá told me."

The full moon illuminates my father as he picks up a tree sprig from the terrace floor and rubs it between his long skinny calloused fingers. I like to listen to my father's stories about his parents, because he did not know them very well, and I only build up an image of their existence through his stories. "Your grandmother Hortensia visited me for months after she died. She would be standing in the kitchen, calling me to put more wood to the stove, and then she would offer me a plate full of cooked rice. Then she would breast-feed a baby. I was only five years old." "Did your other sisters and brother dream about her, too?" I encourage Dad, as his last words trail off. The corners of his eyes wet. He pulls out his handkerchief, blows his nose and steps away. "It is hard for me to remember my life as a child. I didn't know where my brother and sisters were. But this time we are going to win. The *muchachos* are fighting hard in the mountains." Dad is referring to the explosion we heard far away in Guazapa. It is 1980 and the war has broken out ferociously. I adopt the same weakness of voice as he, and looking downward, I say, "Yes, it is sad." He has already walked quite a few steps away from me. I hear him a bit distanced, saying, "This time we are going to win. If in those days we fought with machetes and didn't give up, then this time we use their own weapons to fight the monsters." I know Dad wants to join the guerrilla but he still has eight children to feed, although I and my older two brothers and sister are already trying as much as possible to find our own food resources.

As much as I want to give Dad a really tight hug for trying to give us this mansion, I also recognize that without my mother's persistence to keep him going in the right direction, life would be crazier than it already is. My Father would have been a wandering gypsy or a fisherman in a humble boat, if she had not insisted he build us a real house. She is the equal producer of the cement terrace stories he tells to me. I want to tell him that, even though we nearly drowned in this *barranca*, and even though we temporarily lost almost everything in the hurricane, I feel grateful he built this mansion in the center of the gully he filled in. His crazy ideas about raising us, his children, in the ways of nature are inspiring but uncomfortable. He harvests while my starving imagination tries to glean something meaningful about a past, the present and an unknown future. I am very unsure about hugging people. We don't really hug in our family. If I embrace him now, he might never come back up to the terrace. His mother died when he was five-years-old. He was abandoned at seven years old; he was never baptized; his grandmother burned off his hair, because he ate more than he was supposed to; he never saw his brothers and sisters again until he was an adult. After running away from his grandmother, my father wandered for a few days. He ended up living with a fisherman named Juan Reina in a cave in El Lago de Coatepeque. That is why my father is more affectionate with fish than with us. He passes his calloused hands over fish fins with more ease than over his children's hands, because fishing was his first passion, then construction. Nevertheless, tonight, captured, by the moonlight under this vigil together, a rush of anxiety runs over my hands when I think of the oppressive time the country is going through. Tomorrow I would still have the image of Dad's captured in his silence looking at the light of the moon. I realize that perhaps Dad has been searching for that hug himself as a child, or as an adult all his life. How would he give a hug to us if he never got one himself? He disappears in the darkness under the shadows of the trees, leaving me with all the light of the moon. I look back and he's already going down from the terrace to join Mamá, my sister and brothers in sleep. I go down and go directly to their bedroom and hug both of them, Mamá and Papá. " Ah!...foolish girl." I hear Papá's murmurs from my room that is only divided by plywood and curtains. I laugh quietly.

The Short Cut

My father is known in the *colonia* to be crass and of bad breeding. He doesn't care. A year after the trip to Mexico, Mamá sends me to buy water from the white-dress-uniform girls. By this time, we've lost the vehicle, and our farmlands in Zaragoza. Everything is gone since my father lost his job. Mornings he goes to hunt for a job; afternoons he stays in bed. He says he is tired and needs to sleep. Any noise, any child's error, even the colorless furniture, everything seems to try his patience. When Mamá senses he is about to erupt, she swiftly sends my brother-one-year-younger-than-me to pick *mora* or *chipilin* at the back of the house so she can make soup for Papá, as the green-leaf broth might calm his tightly wrapped frustration.

Sometimes he nails his eyes to the ceiling. I always leave the room before he catches me watching him. The family of the white-dress-uniform-girls is the second family in the *colonia* to connect their house to city water. The only other family with indoor plumbing is the former landowner of the land the *colonia* rests on. "The military helped them get water connections to their house," Papá says. People in the *colonia* label us leftists, *subversivos*, terrorists, communists; the power is now with the *orejas* of the right wing---such a pleasure to turn your neighbors in to be killed. The mother of the white-dress-uniform girls curses us, saying we are going to die and be buried in our own shit. We laugh nervously.

I stand in front of the rectangular mirror hung at the top of the corrugated wall. It is the driver-side mirror with a moon sculpture on it. It is the only thing left from the red Ford pickup Papá had bought from his friend who lives in New Orleans. When he sold the car to Papá, he gave us ten yellow T-shirts that read Michelin Tires. In the mirror I try to arrange my shoulder length hair. The moon on the mirror pisses me off. So I take the hammer and break it off. "What happened?" Mamá calls. "The mirror broke," I yell. "It had to be you," she says swatting and hitting a fly with a snap of her apron.

That year, Papá opens a new path, a shortcut to and from our property. Now we rarely use the main street of the *colonia* to go to the main bus stop. My sister and I avoid the people of the *colonia* by using the shortcut to catch the bus two stops farther along the route to school. The shortcut is dangerous, because it cuts through abandoned land that used to be a *cafetal*. One day we find the naked bodies of two young men with their thumbs tied behind their backs. There are bruises all over their bodies. People say the blackened spots come from electric shocks. Papá prays every night, asking God to save his children from any resentful soul. He is not Catholic, but he carries the Old Testament, just in case there is a God. It doesn't take very long for his fears to come true.

In the middle of the day, I am on my bed in our one-room house reading *The Clandestine Prisons of El Salvador* by Guadalupe Martínez. My eldest brother tears through the living room, flying past me heading toward the exit to the main road. He closes the door silently behind him. Four men with short hair, black sunglasses, and pistols tucked in their pants are close behind him. I run to the outhouse and throw the book into the hole as they search the house. Anyone the authorities find with that book can be killed for reading "subversive" literature.

My brother stays out of the house for a month sleeping in different people's houses, until Papá and Mamá find the money to send him out of the country.They go to Aunt Tona, who wants them to see a shaman or *brujo*. Aunt Tona swears that he makes travelers invisible when they encounter problems on their way. Mamá and Papá listen to her, and consider going to see the shaman. Aunt's Tona's son got to the USA successfully. She says without this *brujo's* help, he could not have gone through the border. Papá and Mamá tell us that if the short cut had not been there, our brother would have been killed by now. The next day, he leaves for Mexico.

Night Memory: The Mansion in the Middle of a Gully

In 1980, I am a theater student at the only arts high school in the country. Every evening I come home from school, eat and then climb a ladder to sit on the cement edge of the unfinished mansion's terrace letting my legs dangle in the air.

Slowly, gradually, I disconnect myself from the problems of our household and the hillside *colonia* where we live. I feel a bit nervous, as though one little bat flits in the pit of my stomach. Fears like thin baby worms cling to my feet, as I look down onto the parched patio. I stare straight off into the faraway city, volcano on my left and hills on my right. I become a large orange kite, a crazy wild thing kids play with. I turn into a bird, a red *guacamaya* with indigo and yellow aspect, feathers flying toward my nest atop the high terrace of the mansion.

On the terrace, this is when and where I really live. Reality these days is a huge armored war vehicle, and I am like that vehicle of traction, like the one that Papá used to start building this half-finished mansion five years ago. I am both conflict and conflicted. Our mansion has become a mausoleum, an ancient Roman ruin jutting out of the earth. It has windows, a lot of them square, and heavy pillars to hold up three stories, strong with heavy walls, and three thick cement ceilings and floors. To look up at me where I sit from down the hill below the house, this must seem like a tall apartment building. But from the street level immediately behind me in the Colonia Rubio, *pelo de elote*, one sees only a one-level house.

When I got off the bus at the bus stop at the edge of the colonia, I heard their comments. "She lives in the house that looks like the cathedral." They are neighbors referring to the cathedral of San Salvador, which is also only half-finished. "I see her sitting on the edge of the building. Maybe she goes up there to pray." Gossip, gossip. I am sure it is the woman who sells tortillas who tells others about the mansion and me. Everyone seems to know about everyone in this neighborhood, this field of ruins. I am learning to detach from ordinary people, since I started art school and began reading art books and history. I read hiding under the bed, eventually paying as much attention to my shadow as to anything else. My shadow is changing from within and has begun to change its outer shape into a young woman.

"It has to be of an Italianate construction to survive earthquakes and hurricanes," Papá says opening a drawing my older brother designed, as a first-year architecture student at the National University. Papá does not really follow the exact design; he has his own plan, square and boxy, but well built. He makes excuses, "What else can one do to turn this gully into a home?" "You're not following our son's design." Mamá criticizes.

The mansion smells of soft new rain and old humidity, as it waits in silence to be whole and complete. Our mansion is not the only unfinished construction site; the whole country looks like ancient Rome, or more like its ruins. At least Rome had its splendor, its glory, and its achievements. Here we have none of these; all is started and left unfinished, unless you are rich.

A 1975 winter of a few years past calls itself forth. Under a September Saturday's yolk-colored sun, the Bee Gees are 'blaming it all' on the "Nights on Broadway" from the shiny marine blue stereo console Papá bought the previous Christmas. He stands at the edge of the newly dug horizontal trench with a rusted shovel in his raised right hand, his left resting on the hammer tucked into the brown belt of his corduroy pants. He calls us, his children, to carry pieces from the rock pile to drop into places he indicates along the long trench. As we watch, he mixes sand, gravel, water, and cement. In turn, he gives us each a shovelful of mixed concrete.

I manage to avoid spilling my shovelful, even though it seems heavier than any rock I've ever carried. He helps each of the littler brothers with a spadeful of concrete. He quickly scoops in the rest of the concrete, and then tells us all to jump into the trench full of wet concrete to stamp on it. He says the wet concrete will kill our foot fungus, although we do not know what foot fungus is, and we are fairly sure we do not have any. A few days later, layers of dead skin peel from our feet. We compete after lunch and after school to see who is faster at peeling off all the dead skin. "Sweep away all the dead skin," Mamá says. "Do not leave it on the floor, because the animals will come inside the house to eat it. You do not want the hens to taste like your feet, do you?" We laugh. Mamá gives us her look; she is not joking.

"We build this mansion in fulfillment of your mother's dream that will be yours, too." Papá says placing a nail between his lips. "Hurry up then," Mamá says sarcastically meaning for him to finish the mansion or at least the task immediately, so they can go buy food. She is dressed to go out, lips colored orange-red. "I am ready to go to the Central Market." But it is his dream, not ours, or maybe we just don't understand. We know Papá never had a home. He ran away from his grandmother's house after his mother and his father died. He was not even seven. (But my paternal grandparents and great grandparents...that is another story). He does not dare call what he is building just a house; he does not even allow us to call it a house, but a mansion, because mansions are what he has built all these years for the rich in their *colonias* farther up in the hills. One day, I suppose it crossed his mind: "Why not build a mansion for myself?"

The Bee Gees' energetic rhythm, the yellow sun, the motion of people passing by the house greeting us from the street, all of it encapsulates for me a moment of confetti- showering, laughing happiness of that Saturday morning, as we imagined a future mansion, that included that day's gentle puffy clouds moving through our blue sky. As Papá spoke and Mamá interrupted him, I swear I could see a bedroom of my own with curtains, lamps, bookshelves, closets, and a table where I sit reading something intelligent.

In 1980, it turns out to be Albert Camus who tries to speak to me from a book on a Thursday evening in September overcast by dark clouds in a rainy month. But 1975 hums within me still. "Hurry up, let's cover the cement or it will all be washed away," Papá hurries to finish the beginnings of a first foundation, under Mamá's slightly impatient gaze. This night memory flashes and is gone. My bedroom might never be finished. Bee Gees' music still sometimes plays on a neighbors' radio, but now its melodic rhythms embitter both past and present. The Mansion is still unfinished. It serves as an emergency barracks for the family, a refuge where we go individually to think up tactics for survival. Mamá takes the immense concrete stairway to the second floor midmornings to dream up strategies to keep us alive through this hell of economic starvation.

The city is gray this evening, like ashes fallen from the sky. This afternoon I was at Parque Libertad waiting for the bus home. There I saw children with their little hands holding Gerber baby food jars to their mouths, inhaling shoe glue. It reminded me the way my little brothers would eat their baby food, spooning it in as fast as they can eat. The label on these baby jars shows a healthy white baby. Is this jar of shoe-glue food for these children, who are usually hidden away in a corner of the park, each child with a baby jar of glue? Their own two hands push it to their mouths. The child sucks and breathes in the poison, dreaming of a bottle of milk they might never have.

In another corner of the park, a young prostitute sells her body to a petty thief. The prostitute is the daughter of the man with the painted face who performs the fire show in *el parque* Libertad every day after five o'clock. The audience drops miserable coins into the hands of the clown's assistant, his daughter. Poor students like me go there for the free entertainment. I like to see the show: the father of the young prostitute takes a bottle of alcohol or gasoline, puts it in his mouth, then, in a single gesture he spits, torches it with a lit match, and spews a cloud of fire, its yellow, orange, purples the same colors as the afternoon horizon of *celajes*. If not for the line of trees at the bottom of the house that has grown up with me, I could see the whole city from the terrace. I wonder where the fire-eating father, his daughter-the-prostitute and the children are sleeping in the park.

I hear steps, definite and slow, come up to the terrace on the old wooden ladder. It is Papá; we are the ones who hold consistent vigil here. That is not entirely true, as I sometimes meet here with my older sister to talk about boys, music, and places around the world to which we would like to escape. "Russia, Costa Rica, Hungary, Czechoslovakia, but Russia for sure!" Then we lie down on the cool humid cement of the terrace to count stars until Mamá reminds us to go to bed no later than ten o'clock.

I look down at the line of white trunks of avocado, coconut and eucalyptus trees on the patio below. Papá whitewashed the bottom half-meter of the tree trunks. I don't know why. Among the trees' fallen decaying brown leaves and branches are two big rust-colored ceramic frogs that someone scavenged for Papá from one of the rich houses he builds. When dead leaves rustle on the ground, I could swear a frog just moved. Everything grows wild here. We've got nothing fancy growing, like the roses or camellias in the gardens of rich people's houses. Here green wild vines climb from the ravines below, where soapy water runs down into the earth to twist tree roots. The trickle of white water flows from my Tía Yita's morning laundering.

I bend my head like a duck to gauge the distance from the top of the terrace to the patio. I grab the terrace's edge with my four fingers like a parrot on its perch. I will not slip accidentally. What would happen if I were to dive from the terrace to the patio? Would I survive the fall as Papá did two years ago? Perhaps not. Papá was very drunk, but I'm not drunk like him. I'm worse than drunk. I am delusional to think I am an artist, an actress without even owning Stanislavsky's actor's manual. I have no money to buy it, and even if I had the money, the book does not even exist in the bookstores in this flea-sized country. Why would I kill myself anyway? Why not just go to *El Cerro de Guazapa* that the *guerrilleros* have taken. I could have gone with el *Cadejo* Negro, as I call my new friend from the Art School, to fight against the armed forces. At least my death would be worth something then. I sigh as I pull myself back from the edge. I try again to measure the distance, but I've never been good at measuring. A ray of moonlight has filtered through the trees, revealing changes in this clod of dirt I have known as home since elementary school.

When my father first brought us to see this piece of land, it was just a littered gully back then. Now the large, solid, unfinished cement house stands in the middle of the shady space, surrounded by maturing fruit trees that were as small as me back then. The mangos, *sunzas*, avocados, and a few leftover coffee trees were already there, before Papá transplanted the others. Now instead of a gully, there is a yard where chickens and ducks sleep. The trees grow, fertilized by memories of recent years and the caca of domesticated birds. The coyotes sometimes scavenge for something to eat in the *barranca*. Tía Yita sets up a small space each evening to sleep close to the trees in case the coyotes attack the hens. Tía Yita knows how to get rid of them. She chants like an owl, or pigeon, or even like a wolf or another coyote. Let them try to eat Tía Yita, I laugh to myself. Those coyotes would be sorry, because she keeps a long eucalyptus stick with a sharp hook like a nail on the end. No animal could escape her strike. The coyotes make me feel the place is haunted with live animals and dead ones, too. I fear the coyotes will carry me away to other ravines where La Siguanaba lives, that wandering madwoman who appears beautiful to men, but once they go with her, she kills them monstrously. That's one story I heard about her.

Where we live is called colonia Rubio. The whole neighborhood's land still bears the name of its original owner, old man *Rubio*, whose name means blond like corn silk. He sold Mamá and Papá this gully as though it were a real piece of land, but it was only a *barranca,* a gully or ravine with coyotes, owls, snakes, some fruit and coffee trees. Whenever it rained, the whole gully filled like a lake. My father hauled tons of earth and put three heavy stone walls and another foundational wall to create some real land. He was sure to divide it from another barranca next to us that was also full of coffee and orange trees. That gully still belongs to the colonia owner Rubio.

The first year we came to the colonia, a hurricane hit the whole country. It was one o'clock in the morning, when our beds were floating in different directions. Mamá carried my two little brothers, a three-month-old baby, and a one-year-old. Papá was not there. He was building a mansion somewhere else in another part of the country. The Formica table, a big rusty frying pan, the water barrels and ourselves were all we rescued from that disaster.

"As long we are alive, we can always start over," Mamá said while making a fire when the rain lightened on the only flat piece of land up close to the so-called Main Street. Four strong wood poles, mango tree branches and a corrugated metal roof were what my older brothers managed to put back up during the hurricane. The neighbors closest to our barranca brought us coffee and bread. The whole colonia was wrecked, but we did not have a house. Even the house we had before the hurricane was improvised, anyway.

When Papá came home the next night, it was still raining the last of the hurricane. He brought with him two of his old coworker friends, el Chato Nicolás, and el Chele Pavián. Tío Polo, Tía Yita's husband, showed up, too, without letting us know ahead of time, as if there were a way to let us know they were coming. The hurricane summoned Papá and Tío Polo back to our house. Tío Polo worked at another construction site that Papá also managed. The bigger fallen mango tree branches served as a good roof structure during the last of the rains. Papá directed us to hang sheets of plastic over the branches and leaves to form an enormous umbrella. Three days after father's return, by the third morning we had a new solidly improvised house, as Papá, el Chato, el Chele Pavián, Tío Polo and my older brothers worked even at night.

This temporary house was stronger and bigger, so my Tía Yita and my two cousins could be with us to help in the next catastrophe. It is not that Tía Yita was far away from us when the hurricane happened. Her settlement was close to our *barranca*. We heard her screaming for help with her two children on top of her back as water and mud pulled at her, as she held on to a mango tree. Papá and Mamá decided to leave everything buried, as the mud was too thick and deep to find the rest of our belongings.

From the mansion terrace I look down at the dirt patio and wonder how long it will take to finish this mansion. It is 1980, and Papá has lost his construction employment. A war has broken out throughout the country. We are living on the savings Mamá had hidden away. They sold the land they owned to make a farm outside the city to keep us all alive. Papá is here with me on the terrace. We sit together quietly. The silence between us inspires us to excavate memory. "Do you remember when we first came to this colonia?" Papá asks me, gazing at the moon over the hills of Guazapa. "Yes," I say. I ask him, "do you remember when you said, 'We'll be fine?' that's what you said before the hurricane hit us." "Hija, war scars the soul worse than any natural catastrophe. Men are killing each other." I follow his gaze.

Do we build up future like we built up this barranca? How does one do that? I wonder whether Papá knows which hammer and nail to take...and I wonder how to take the right path to the center of this labyrinthine universe where children are homeless, where the unprotected sell their bodies, where women cry for their disappeared, and elders suffer strokes and heart attacks because of ceaseless worry for food and for their children. Sons and daughters are leaving to save their own lives from disaster here. They flee violence, look for better lives and a just society. Mamá calls Papá and me. It is time to sleep.

1975 speaks to me still, and I swear I can no longer see the bedroom with curtains, lamps, bookshelves, closets, and a table. Instead, I read something intelligent as I sit on the terrace of my brothers', sisters' and my unfinished mansion.

The White-Dress-Uniform-Girls

The girls who live diagonally across from my house go to school at *El Central de Señoritas*. They wear uniforms, like virgin nurses in white dresses. At age sixteen, I wear Levis and a baggy blouse. They stand about a meter behind me computing, measuring, blueprinting, and recording all my movements and words as I talk with my drama teacher and two other art students. Once they are home, they will tell their mother about me. They undoubtedly will say they saw me with three men--- one older, weird-looking man with a long beard who looks like a communist. Their mother will pass this gossip on to Nata, the storeowner who offers credit to everyone in the *colonia*.

Nata in wide-eyed amazement tries continually to find out whose girls in the *colonia* have begun to menstruate. "Martita, she is already moving her tail when she sees boys around, or when they are parked on the street whistling at the girls. There she goes with her tight pants and wet long black hair to see whether she'll get her whistle. Today she came to buy a package of Kotex. I think it's for her and not for her mother. The poor mother became an Evangelic to save her youngest daughter. Her other daughters left her, all three of them pregnant by who knows who. The girls from the street above, the twin sisters of *Plomadita*, already have the red river flowing through their lives. Very soon we'll see them with babies in their arms like their sister."

Nata says variations of this to each woman who comes to buy from her. My dad says Nata needs a man to keep her busy. Nata tells Mamá she once had a love, and a son, and now they are both gone. Anyway, once you share gossip with Nata, she acts as the news anchor for the neighborhood, although she is more careful with what she says about me or my brothers and sisters, because of her friendship with Mamá, whose temper can melt metal. Nata is known in the *colonia* as *El Diario de Hoy* because of the lies both say.

Claudia is the mother of the girls-in-white-dresses. She works washing military uniforms at a military headquarters. Her husband, Paco, was a driver for the Humberto Romero family. Romero was the president thrown out of office in 1979. Papá says 1979 was the last year of the fat cows, the end of the decade of Salvador's economic growth. That same year Paco worked on weekends sometimes as my father's driver to take us places. Apparently the Romero family stopped needing a driver. We became *"friends"* with the white-dress-uniform girls.

One day, when I was about twelve years old, on a trip to Santa Ana, Papá gets very drunk and laughingly says to Mamá, "Look, Rosita! These sons of bitches, they're the Anemic family." He points to Paco and Claudia. "The military has left you guys anemic. They have sucked out all your blood...anemic sons of bitches." Papá is crazy like this whenever he has *Espíritu de Caña* in his mouth. That day Papá stands on a curb in front of the Santa Ana cathedral, lifts the bottle to the blue sky, and blesses the liquor. *"Vino que del cielo vinó,"* he incants and sprays some drops on the cement street. "For those who died thirsty for wine and love." We children sit on the curb waiting for Papá to finish the bottle. The white-dress-uniform girls and their mother lean on one side of the pickup, their faces wrinkled up like old ripe mangos, bored with the moment or perhaps their lives.

I think the white-dress-uniform girls are only happy when they watch soap operas like *Mundo de juguetes*. When I was about seven years old, I would observe them smiling at me whenever I would go buy water right after the soap opera would finish. I would wonder, "Is it *Mundo de Juguetes?* No, it must be a different soap opera now. *Mundo de juguetes* finished a long time ago. I don't know what the current soap opera is."

When I was little, I used to watch soap operas at lunch time through the hole in the door of a neighbor's home. My brother-one-year-younger-than-me and I used to take turns watching through the hole. "Hurry up! It's my turn. Move," he would say. "Wait," I say, "they are kissing now. You're not allowed to see that." We do not have a TV yet, and *Mundo de juguetes* is the hot topic for the girls and their mothers at school. Sometimes I pretended to know all about soap operas when talking with the girls at school. My mother, my sisters and sometimes I must have seemed like strange creatures since we never really talk about soap operas. Mamá seemed to end most conversations with, "Umm, eh, I have to go. Antonio is waiting for his *queso con chile*. Bye."

The protagonist of *Mundo de Juguetes* is a beautiful rich girl named Cristina. She suffers because her rich father lost her mother in a tragic accident, and he can't find another woman like her. A woman who is innocent, beautiful, smart, a good mother, a good wife, and a good boss to servants is apparently difficult to find. He marries the nun from his daughter's school. I remember when Cristina runs away because her father doesn't let her bring a homeless person--- or is it a lost dog?--- to live with them. All the girls from the *colonia* are sad. I pretend to be sad too. We talk about poor Cristina and hope nothing happens to her on the dangerous streets of Mexico, or is it Venezuela? That is also the day the neighbors' son, *Chele* William, is raped, but we are so worried about Cristina we don't think about him. I never find out how poor rich Cristina's story ends, because the neighbors seal up the hole in the door.

The younger white-dress-uniform girl is Silvia, but ever since *Mundo de juguetes,* everyone calls her Cristina. One day I ask her why. "Don't you see I look like Cristina? And my complete name is Silvia Cristina," she tells me and sings the show's theme song as she rubs her long pigtails. "But Cristina is rich and is a beautiful girl." I say this from a little distance, ready to run away in case she cries for her mother and sister to come out to throws stones at me. "But I have a new set of dishes and dolls, and I go to a better school than you. I have clean nails. I don't play with imaginary toys like you. I don't steal mangos from the neighbors' yards. I have many pairs of shoes. Your brothers and sisters always run around barefoot, and your mother is a rabbit because she is always having babies." She recites this to me as though she has practiced it. I pull her pigtails as she finishes reciting, and my older sister and little brothers join me. We all pull her pigtails and make her kiss the ground. My brother-one-year-younger-than-me sticks his naked foot in her mouth. She starts crying, and her mother and sister come out with knives and

148

stones. We retreat to our house, lock the doors, and watch them from our single long rectangular window.

Tía Yita gets mad with us. My aunt is afraid of this family, because they're crazy. They don't like us. When we get into fights with them, they have family allies who take to the street in front of our house and throw rocks, stones, garbage and water at us. "Savages, your parents and you will all burn in hell." Mamá and Papá are never home in the afternoon, so Tía Yita takes care of us. My aunt tends to side with the family of the white-dress-uniform girls because they give my cousin Carmen used clothes and broken dolls. Tía Yita comes outside and meets with them, and promises she will tell Mamá and Papá to punish us. When Mamá comes home, Tía Yita tells her about the fight. That night, Papá whips us with his belt on our bare legs---my sister and me twice, because we're older than the others. My two older brothers are always working, at school, or out with girlfriends. My sister and I make a pact to break Silvia's new set of dishes the next time she leaves them in the patio where she plays.

Four years later, my family and Silvia Cristina's family stand under a hot sky waiting for Papá to finish his bottle. We sweat like pigs. Silvia, who is about twelve years old like me, stands next to her mother, Claudia, who leans against the side of the pickup. Her sister, Maria, now sits inside the pickup cabin with her father at the steering wheel. They are like stones. In front of the Santa Ana cathedral the *paletero* stops his cart to ring the bell. *"Paletas de mango con leche, coco con leche, de nueces, zapote y mamey."* We salivate. He removes the cover of the ice cream cart, and a little brother gets a *mango con leche*. My sister, brothers and I ask my father for money to buy popsicles. We never ask Mamá, because she never gives us money. I invite the white-dress-uniform girls, but they just scrunch up their faces. I think they still hate us, perhaps more now that we have a car and they don't. It is March and the devil's hour, as people call twelve o'clock noon. The heat has flushed a pomegranate color on my cheeks and my sister's, brothers' and Mamá's. Papá raises again and again the bottle of liquor to his mouth. Why doesn't he catch fire in this sun? The other white-dress-uniform girl, Maria, steps out of the pickup cabin to rejoin her sister and mother at the side of the pickup. They don't look like us. Their cheeks don't have color, although the red-hot orange ball is right on them, too. "You see, you and your family look like anemic mummies. Not even the sun wants to share its color with you, because you have sold your soul to the militaries. You're sons of bitches…" Papá yells these lines into the air, just as he finishes the last drop of liquor.

Mamá springs into action. In one breath, she calls us to get in the back of the pickup, pushes Papá into the front seat of the pickup, sits inside as well, and apologizes to Paco. Besides being angry with my father, Mamá is scared of the soldiers who stand with their rifles around the cathedral. The rest of us get into the back of the pickup. The white-dress-uniform girls and their Mom shut their eyes and their mouths as though they have been stuffed with cotton balls.

I never again spend time with the white-dress-uniform girls. Already we are in high school, I see them only on the bus going home. Sometimes when I come home for lunch, we get off at the same stop at the top of the colonia. I walk behind them, all the way home. When I get inside the house, I see them turn back and throw me a look, as though they might want to ask me something about my weird friends, or perhaps they want to be my friends again, but their mother would punish them, since we are branded neighborhood leftists. My sister and I and the girls-in-white-dresses are all teenagers now, but they still look like the little girl from the soap-operas of *Mundo de jugetes*. I respond to their thrown look by waving to them before they get inside the gate of their home. The mother comes out and glares down our street. Are we still at war?

…after…CAROLINA RIVERA ESCAMILLA

La Carnada/The Bait

In her last year of high school, the only change Dalia makes is to sneak into adult movies. Watching movies gives her other lives, other homes, and other hopes that feel bigger than this city, surrounded by soldiers and death. To get into the X-rated movies, she wears eyeliner to look older. After all, she is studying theater and needs to practice camouflaging her age. One of the older boys in drama class tells her during lunch that he sometimes goes to the movies at the Metro Cinema, behind *el parque Libertad*. She has seen the marquees with images of beautiful, exuberant half-dressed women with a lot of eye makeup and breasts swelling out of their bras. Before she passes the cinema, she tries to see what's playing from far away, so that the passersby won't mistake her for some pervert.

Around the middle of the school year, Dalia decides to accompany the boys at lunchtime to the movies. She checks out the marquee ahead of time. *La Carnada* matinee plays at 11:45 am. In the poster she sees a woman in her thirties with straight black long hair, dark eyes and a heart-shaped face sitting with her legs spread on a chair, a pencil behind her ear. Under the chair is a muscular, dark-haired, handsome guy, looking at her legs in a lustful way. In the background of the same poster, there is a smaller version of the actress sitting on a bicycle in sexy short shorts and a tiny blouse with her breasts bulging. This time the pencil is between her lips. In this picture the handsome guy is seated behind her on the bike with a malicious-yet-pleasant smile. He is looking into the camera. Dalia feels as though he is looking at her. At the bottom of the poster it reads: *"una pelicula italiana que le pone la carne de gallina."* She returns to school and tells the guys that she will go with them at lunchtime to see *La Carnada*. One of the boys calls her over to a corner of the classroom to convince her to change her mind.

"Why?" She says.

"The movie is only for men, older men," he says and puts his hands in his pockets.

"I am going. I know what Italian movies are like. They have

152

funny stuff, and romance, and they are scary. This movie is scary because it says that it will give you goose bumps."

"Fine, come with us, but don't get scared when the boys do boys' stuff." He smiles and returns to his seat. She pictures all of them having sex with female aliens in the dark movie theater. Dalia asks Ana and Alba to accompany her. They are happy to be invited, especially since she pays for them. Otherwise, they couldn't go. She doesn't usually have money, but she has been saving her bus money, walking home for a week, and skipping lunch.

The seven of them walk to the Metro Cinema, a new movie theatre in the heart of the city. Young punks and drug addicts hover at the entrance of the building. It is amazingly dark even though it is almost midday. She scrutinizes the ticket line; they are mostly men in their thirties and forties. There are some strange looking couples. She assumes the women might be prostitutes, because they match the way her Papá describes them badly dressed, in bad shape, improper behavior with their bodies. The men who accompany them look like *maleteros*, men who work in the heart of the city shining shoes or street-sellers or maybe even vagrants. Three of the couples in the middle of the line look decent, in clean suits, ties, shiny shoes, the women dressed like the secretaries from *El Banco Salvadoreño*, the bank where many Salvadorans with money have accounts.

Why am I dressed in overalls today? she wonders and asks Ana for lipstick. Ana laughs and hands it to her. She doesn't have a mirror, so Alba puts some on her lips before they get to the ticket window.

"One ticket," She says to the tough-looking, dark-skinned man. He's about forty and his front tooth is crowned of gold fill.

"You're too young for *La Carnada*," he says to Dalia and looks at the next customer in line.

"I need to see the movie. It's homework for my art class. They are also from my class," she insists as she points to the group.

"Yes, sir. It is an art project," one of the boys says. The man impatiently sells each of them a ticket.

They sit in the same row, the three girls together and the boys to their right. The movie opens with the beautiful exuberant woman from the poster coming to visit her teenage nephew.

Twenty minutes later, there is already intercourse, oral sex, foot sex, masturbation, and a lot of moaning inside the cinema. Dalia's two girlfriends' legs tense up like hers, and she feels her vagina moistening involuntarily. The handsome actor is under the table on all fours with his head inside the actress's crotch. When she sees the man's tongue inside the actress's vagina, she gets up and leaves, and the other two girls leave, too. The boys stay.

They walk into the daylight, so pale and bright, full of people going somewhere, anywhere. Ana and Alba have to go in the opposite direction to take the bus home. Dalia pretends she is going home, but instead she goes to Lourdes café, a few blocks from the Metro cinema to wait for the guys. When they pass the café, she yells one of the boys' name. They join her for a few minutes and tease her for not staying until the end of the movie. Although they laugh, their faces look pale and tense. She never goes to Metro Cinema again.

...after...CAROLINA RIVERA ESCAMILLA

The Bed

Each time the blows resounded on the door of his mother's house, he ran to hide under his childhood bed. That's how life had been for two weeks since he got cut off from the Guerrilla organizations after the final offensive at the end of January 1981. The year would be decisive for the country and for him, for those people who wanted change, the year of the offensive, the year of the revolution of the reddening moon that would lay out hundreds of barely armed high school and university students into the gutters of San Salvador.

His mother had told him that Carlos, with whom he had escaped soldiers in hilly Colonia Escalón, had been captured in those days when summer wind moves moaning tree branches, the month of January 1981. The soldiers' leaden eyes were searching, and they followed Carlos to his home. They took him out and burned him alive along with his girlfriend in front of families to bind them with fear. Streets of the capital breathed in repression through the barrel of a rifle and were camouflaged in olive green, where most young people walked as though drawn by wires so as not to raise any suspicion.

They knock on the door again; he hides; they leave. Now lying on the floor he examines rusty springs and wonders how long it will take them to find him, and how he will flee from this. The streets are dressed with soldiers and whistle-blowing informants. Just stepping out of the house, they'll shoot him down. "How stupid. How could I come home for Mamá to hide me?" There was no other safe place at the time. Surrounded in that house, he is a fugitive in his own home, an exile in his own country. "Mamá will not let me go."

There, from under his bed, he also sees the ceiling of his house, where he once dreamed that the sky was a blackboard on which girls and boys painted a rainbow, where they learned to read and write. This is the bed he and his brother shared when he started storing memory at five years of age. A memory flourishes of playing the game of cat and mouse, of hide and seek. They never caught him, but now he was not so sure of his game, and the cat was not his brother. These cats have become vultures with rifles.

"Stop, stop jumping. You're going to break the bed, and then you'll have to go back to sleeping on the floor like before. There is no money to buy another. Look, the mattress is already torn." He hears his young mother's voice yelling at them. He sighs guiltily at the memory of her scolding dissolves. Completely still, his fingers feel the space where his father set up the bed fifteen years ago. With a thin smile and one eye half-open looking up at the mattress, he realizes why he felt backaches every morning about which he never complained, because the pains were never as strong as the joy of having a bed with mattress; that was greater than any annoying spring touching his back. "The springs of this thin mattress were almost touching my face. Mother must have put things on the bed to hide me better when they get here."

He hears again violent knocking and feels there is no escape. He can reach out to touch his mother's weak, nervous pacing. She has enough force to get to the door. Lying on the icy floor of interwoven red and green bricks he enjoys momentarily as the peach-colored light of noon seeps through the crack in the door his mother barely lets open. Filtering through the light come three violent shadows that push the door against mother.

He becomes silent as the icy floor where he lies. Courage becomes thin as the mattress where he has slept since he was five. Watch the evil black boots, hungry for searching. They are the mocking vultures, pecking with hate at the home to find him. In seconds, the bed goes crash flying across the room. He feels as if naked without it. He does not move. His mother cries. A rifle butt silences her. He lies there, face toward the ceiling, still as though the bed is still upon him. He does not feel the blow of rifle butt on his face. Nor does he feel his head when they crash it on the edge of the bed. They drag him. Would he sleep in his bed or dream again?

… *after*…

It is after the assassination of Archbishop Monseñor Oscar Arnulfo Romero.

It is after the end of the rainy season, the end of October.

It is after the school year ends.

It is after the American nuns are raped, shot and buried at the side of a road, out of sight of the airport.

It is after the massacre of students at the Universidad de El Salvador, who were bombed and burned alive in the tunnels they themselves had dug under the university to hide weaponry from the military, tunnels where they thought they might hide, too.

It is after the first guerilla uprising. It is soon after the government's decision to have the death squads leave body parts in neighborhoods, to create fear and intimidation.

It is after our Papá loses his job forever as a master builder, because he refuses to leave the workers' union.

It is after he is swallowed up by the daily drinking he cannot stop.

It is after the first Christmas the family spends without our three oldest boys.

It is after our parents force them to flee to Mexico because they are politically involved, because there is no way for young men to avoid being conscripted from the streets, because there is no work here, and because our father and mother cannot feed us all.

It is after our father says to the eldest, "Take this money. Tomorrow we wake up at four in the morning. We are leaving. I am dropping you at the border of Guatemala and Chiapas." He says, "God go with you. Don't forget us." A few months, then a year later he repeats the same scene with my second oldest and then my third oldest brothers. We get up early and give each brother a hug. Each time our mother attempts to weep quietly, but it is too hard for her. The wrinkles around our father's eyes grow more obvious, deeper each time the ritual is repeated.

It is after my father and uncle spend a whole day going from the jail in Santa Ana to the prison in San Salvador, looking for cousins who had been taken away the night before because some *orejas* say these young men from the countryside are with the guerilleros.

It is after our father and uncle return to Santa Ana that next day to be told that clear plastic bags, with tops carefully tied with plastic-coated wire have been found discarded on the street in Santa Ana. The bags contain the disassembled bodies of two young males.

It is after our uncle identifies his sons from their gold dental work and a ring left on a finger.

It is after I fall in love with a guerillero. He says, "Let's meet at the *el Parque Libertad* tomorrow at eight a.m. Then I will take you to a house where other compañeros and I are hiding." Orlando wants to hold me in his arms. I take his hand and give it a squeeze to say yes. When we arrive at the house the next day, not in the morning but at dusk, I see the house has no electricity, no water. He says, "We are careful to enter and exit unnoticed, at night only, for a few days at a time. Then we move on to another secret location." There are only a few blankets on the tile floor. "Sit down and don't open any windows," he whispers to me after we climb through a back window. "And don't go into the other room." He smiles at me. "There's a very fat man, a very strange person living there."

As he walks towards the bathroom, I notice the open door to the other room. I've been told not to, but I go in and find the floor covered with Spanish newspapers from 1930 to 1935. There are boxes of books, medals and antique bullets on shelves. There are pictures of military men from that era on the walls. Everything in the room is related to the civil war in Spain. I feel strange as I think of Spain, and then of Europe and its subsequent holocaust.

An arm reaches around my waist, and I let out a short scream. "I told you not to come over here!" Orlando smiles, grows serious as he holds his index finger to my lips.

"Shhh... We are only here for a few days to do a special task and then we will go to another place. Who knows where?" he hugs me, kisses me so hard that I feel I am disappearing into him in that dark room.

It is after my friend Alba's family found her body on San

Francisco Street in the neighborhood of Jardines de Guadalupe. Her breasts had been hacked off and a stick was shoved into her vagina. The death squads liked to dump bodies in this quiet stretch of neighborhood where children take short cuts to and from school.

It is after my sister Estela starts having visions of evil shadows at the window and takes to her bed for six months. I spend hours and hours at her bedside consoling her.

It is after my father comes home very drunk from a day's search for a job that doesn't exist. He breaks the television, all the light bulbs in the house and then some furniture. With our mother we hide from him under the beds until he passes out. Then, we tie him to the side of his wooden bed until the next morning.

It is after the guerillas' final offensive. I say goodbye to Orlando and never see him again.

It is after I finish my high school studies and my mother makes me a white cotton jumpsuit for the graduation ceremony, but I am not able to wear it because I spill coffee on it at breakfast. "Damn it, girl! Just because you don't like it doesn't mean you have to do that." My mother starts crying. I wear an old pair of my brother's pants and a boy's shirt. At graduation, the Director of the Ministry of Education says, "I am very happy to honor our successful art students, who, with such great effort, have completed their secondary education." Certificates are passed out to each of us, and we are asked to pose for a picture. In the class photo there are five other girls in dresses and I look like a boy, with a big smile. One of the girls is pregnant. I roll up my certificate and stick it in my pants pocket. The graduation party is at one of the boys' homes. His mother is cooking a pig to celebrate.

It is after I find myself looking for a job on the streets of San Salvador, and instead of finding a job, I have men stopping their cars to ask me if I want to hop in. From a distance, I yell, "Pig! Hijos de puta!" and I feel better.

It is after one of my former teachers asks me to join a guerrilla movement.

"Which group do you want to go with? El Bloque Popular Revolucionario? LP 28? FAPU? AES? There's a war going on."

He knows my well-practiced ability to involve myself and still not commit. "You can't just *pretend* to be part of everything, you have to choose a group to belong to. You must take sides." He says this in a solid sure voice, aware of my confusion about what each group represents.

"Yes, then LP 28," I say, and shortly thereafter I'm trained to use a .38 caliber gun and I learn response tactics in case I'm apprehended by government forces. I am given basic tasks to help the struggle, like distributing pamphlets or speaking at high schools about the conflict. I encourage their creation of graffiti signs.

It is after I become a mature self-conscious revolutionary at the ripe age of eighteen that I find I have the power to speak up for others.

It is after I feel as though I am being asphyxiated by the troubles of this world. I am so tired of all the shit happening, of listening to the growling of my empty stomach, of abandoned street children asking me for money, of seeing mothers, burdened to the point of breaking, because they cannot find their disappeared sons and daughters.

It is after I meet Elvis at National Symphony Hall, where I finished my theater studies, and where I still practice with a theater group in the evenings. When the military attacks and destroys the National Art School, they claim it has become a site for the storage of weapons and a school to train guerrillas. The day they come in, they put us all down on the floor. The school goes silent for the entire morning. Then we are released. The next day when we return, it has been destroyed. Paint, easels, mirrors, make-up, brushes are everywhere. Teachers and we art students discuss whether to go into exile, which means finding other spaces to continue classes, especially for the theater students. I finished my secondary school in different sites: The Music School for academic classes in the morning and the National Theater in the afternoon, and some days we are in the Symphony Building.

I see the long skinny lonely shadow of Elvis every evening through the clouded glass door of a rehearsal cubicle practicing *Fuegos Artificiales de Handel* on his violin. Once after theater practice, I knock on his door.

161

"Can I help you?" he says standing very straight. He is wearing stonewashed jeans with a plaid shirt carefully tucked in it. He is holding both his violin and bow in his right hand. On his left shoulder is a piece of cloth, like a handkerchief, where he rests the violin. I have seen other violinists do that.

"Hi, I like what you are playing. I practice theater upstairs." His big, dark almond-shaped eyes stare at me, as though I am bothering him so I say goodbye and walk away. When I turn around, he is still standing in the doorway. As I leave the building, I turn around for one last glance, sure he has retreated to his cubicle, away from the world and from me. To my surprise he is still watching me. Now I really rush away from the silenced building.

Late one afternoon I arrive at school, come around the building and he is playing *Fuegos Artificiales* again, but I continue upstairs to find my theater friends. No one is there; the building is quiet, except for the sound of secretaries' casual conversations over the tapping of typewriters. As I walk down the stairs to leave, Elvis stands in the shadowy middle of the stairway landing, cradling his violin. I think he might be smiling, but when I listen carefully, I think he might be crying. I rush past him down the stairs without saying a word.

"Hi, my name is Elvis," he calls to my back. "How come you are not greeting me today?" I stop. I turn around in the middle of the long empty Grand Hall. Mornings the symphony practices here and musicians have left their instruments along the walls. Sometimes I sit and listen to symphony rehearsals. One day I imitate the director for a few seconds as he conducts, and his players laugh, and I run fast upstairs.

I say, "So today you're talking to me?"

"You didn't give me a chance last time. You walked away."

"You're a strange person."

He smiles. "You're an actress?" He moves toward me.

Elvis and I become friends. We go up on the roof of the symphony building every evening to talk about politics, literature, philosophy, music and arts. We watch San Salvador and spy on the funeral home nearby where daily, more dead soldiers are carried in on stretchers. One evening Elvis plays his violin on the roof and I dance along, but we leave quickly, never

162

to return after we spy on two military men who hand something to a man in front of the funeral home. We recognize the man as the janitor of the symphony building. From then on, I only feel safe practicing in the mornings. Elvis changes his practice schedule after the janitor tries to knife him one evening in his cubicle. Elvis escapes from the janitor. He cannot be certain whether the janitor is drunk or just pretending to be drunk. He only knows the janitor waited until everyone left the building before confronting him in his cubicle.

It is after the theater group disbands because the war keeps us from being able to perform. The National University becomes the place to meet my friends. My sister and I enter university to study in the law department, as do many other students in the arts. After practicing his music, Elvis comes in the afternoons to meet us at the cafeteria. My sister and our friends find him strange, but accept him because he is my friend. These days we are all a little strange, as we have to screen everyone to make sure he or she is not an *oreja*, "a spying ear." But Elvis is apolitical and strange. I like him because he plays the violin well. He is confused about life.

I leave university after I flunk an economics test. I accompany Elvis to his rehearsals, to his French classes, and to performances at churches where he gets paid to play the piano for weddings. We only have enough money for bad cups of coffee. I've heard of Lattes and Espresso, I've never had one. We dream that one day we will have the normal lives of young people, but we realize that might have to happen in a far away country. Russia is where I hear that most things are fair and just, and where art is the best. Then we go to Elvis' place—an apartment close to the university paid for by his parents —and he plays the violin for me, *fuegos artificiales*, of course. He has a red, red wine, and plays a popular song in English called *Lady in Red*. As he plays, his neck bends to his left side where he places the violin.

He draws a pencil portrait of me and writes letters and drawings on the borders of the white page that explain why we should not have sex. I know he's afraid. The word God scares him. My political position scares him. His parents are making all his decisions for him. There are no jobs for artists and young people. But I like how he plays his violin and he writes me long letters. We are still going for cheap coffee whose color reminds me of the hot water with oregano Mamá gives me during painful menstrual periods. Over weak cups of coffee we kiss and kiss but never consummate. We challenge each other with denials of love. Nothing is secure and I refuse to trust. We say we will only marry people from other worlds. It seems as though we spend a year like this. Elvis flunks out of his private Jesuit university, the UCA, or Universidad Centro Americana, José Simeón Cañas. He is twenty-five years old. I am nineteen.

It is after I find myself trapped by the past, stuck in a hopeless present, looking for any kind of a future. Through the open window of our old house, I see my mom seated on the spiral cement stairway of the unfinished house and I go to sit with her.

"Why are you crying, Mamá? What's the matter?" Like her I sit with my hands folded on my lap. She doesn't answer. I look at the bird that has stopped on the windowsill. I look around at the cement construction my father started building nine years ago. Will he ever finish it? When he began the house, my father would hug my mom and say, laughing, "All twelve of my children will live here, a bedroom for each one. It will look like a castle, with all my grandchildren." It is a three-story house, the biggest in the Colonia. Now it's a cold empty place we go to be alone. Neighbors call it "the Cathedral," referring to the cathedral of San Salvador, which is not finished either, maybe, because of the civil war. After the assassination of Archbishop Romero the cathedral became a blood-spilling ground. Like the Catholic cathedral at the heart of San Salvador, our family's cathedral house is a place of tears, sadness, doubts, debts, and especially my parent's constant anguish because they don't know where to get their children's daily bread.

"Mamá, what's the matter?"

"We have sold everything. Your father can't get a job. We haven't heard anything from your brothers. We don't even know whether they got across the border to Chiapas into Mexico, or if they are going on to the United States." Mamá weeps hard, and covers her face with her hands. I want to cry, too, but no tears come out.

"I know, Mamá. Look at me. I am nineteen, almost twenty years old, and I can't even help the family. I just hope my brothers are all right in Mexico, or wherever they are." I have learned to suppress the crying. I stand up straight and go down a few steps.

"We don't have food for today. We owe money to the market. Your little brothers have no shoes, no clothes to go to school. We spent all our money to send your brothers to Mexico, and they haven't sent us anything, not even a letter."

I have been reading about what it is like going north. I say, "It is not easy to cross the border to the other side. For my brothers it will be harder because they are not Mexicans, so the Mexican police can just take them and put them in jail, if they are lucky. Besides, the US doesn't want Salvadorans there. They think we are just America's back yard, where they dump what they do not want and take what is good for them from here. Look, they are the ones sending billions of dollars to destroy the guerrilla movements here." I am very sure of myself, looking straight into her face. "My brothers should come back and join the struggle here." "Don't say that! Your brothers could be killed just like your cousins." "I miss them so much," she tells me. It has been five years since I have seen them, and I feel I will lose all of you the same way." My mother is losing the struggle to control her emotions.

It is after I tell her, "I miss them, too. I won't leave you, Mamá."

It is after I write a letter to the Canadian consul in Costa Rica asking for political asylum.

It is after I lie to her. She says, "You feel as though you are so far away from us. You do whatever you want. You stay out too late at nights, never asking us. You don't eat here. You don't ask for anything from us like your sisters and brothers. Do you hate us?" Mamá gestures for me to sit with her on the stairs. We sit very close to each other. "No, Mamá, not at all! I could never hate you, or Papá or my brothers and sisters. You are everything for me, but what am I supposed to ask for? There is no money. Look at you. You used to buy shoes to match your dress and even your lipstick before. I feel bad that you can't do those things now." I feel ashamed for not being more expressive with them, for not appreciating their struggle to keep us alive.

"Your father and I would have been happy to see you finish

university and to see you pursuing your dreams. I would love to give you what you need as woman, but this war is destroying any dreams we had for you all. I will never forget this war as long as I live!"

It is after she pulls a letter out from her dress. She usually puts things in her bra, believing them safer there than anywhere else. She hands me the letter. "What is it?" I ask surprised.

"It is a letter from the Canadian Consul in Costa Rica. It came this morning. I opened it. Now it seems you are leaving us, too." Her voice quavers. I am lying when I tell my mother, "I don't have to go."

It is after weeks of being followed from the University by strange men in dark glasses. They appear behind me as I walk to the bus stop. When I get on the bus, my shadow escorts watch me from the back. One day, I lose them by getting off at the wrong bus stop. I slip out at the last minute and watch their confusion, staring at me through the bus' back window as the bus pulls away. Now they know I have recognized them and tomorrow I will have a different pair of spies on my trail until the routine is repeated.

My mother says, "You are free to go. I always have this idea of you as a bird anyway. When you were nine years old, you came to me saying, 'Mamá, I want to fly away,' and I said we are going to make some wings for you when your father comes home, and he designed a bird costume with cardboard wings for you, and you would fly all around the house. Now you will fly away with real wings." She gets up from the steps. "Come on, let's give the news to your brothers and sisters."
I try to explain, "Wait, I am only leaving because..." I want to tell her about the disappearances of friends, and how afraid I am for my own life. But I shut my mouth. I decide not to tell her. What good will it do? She will only be more worried. I glance around the half-finished construction site that is my father's uninhabitable castle. Finally, I read the letter.

Elvis comes by the house at five p.m. to say goodbye to me. When our conversation lasts so long he ends up staying the night with us. Mamá and Papá make sure to put us in separate spaces. Mamá makes sure she can see me in my sister's bed where I usually sleep.

From my bed I can hear Mamá and Papá talking quietly. I cannot hear the words, but I am sure it is about my trip, and feeling worry once again about me (a daughter) going to an unknown place. It is not okay for the boys to go either, but they can go. As for the girls, as much as I tell them it is not their fault, they still feel more guilt about us. When the roosters call I realize I have not slept at all. The night should have lasted many more hours, but the roosters know their hour.

Elvis and I go up the wooden ladder to the terrace of the unfinished mansion. We stare into the barely birthing yellow-orange horizon behind the trees. He is quiet. We talk about the funeral home. I recall a lesson from theatre class. I watch us through my mind's eye in four stages: I see me, both as me and as a spectator; I see our trees, the city; and then the horizon at the back. I take a long, deep breath like an actor before her first entrance onto the stage. I fill my belly with air, then slowly I let it go...and I wonder when I am going to see and feel this horizon again, with the scent of June's morning mangos.

Elvis smiles, "Just consider this as another theatre rehearsal in your life. I know that I'll write to you, and that you might not answer my letters, or that you might answer only one. I'll miss you, but...just go." Our eyes meet for a moment as the chatter of a flock of parrots passes overhead on their flight to San Salvador Volcano. It is after six o'clock in the morning.

It is after I hear voices hurry like a small stream down our main street of compacted dirt. We climb down the wooden ladder to meet Mamá, Papá, my sisters, my aunts and little brothers. Like them, I feel the anxious silence. We are all touched by the long sighs of my aunts' soft mutterings: "Ay, no, se nos va tan lejos." "Oh no, she's going so far away." The children ask, "Where is Canada?"

We hear the motor of the old pickup outside. It will transport us to the airport. The smiling face and small, slender eyes of El chino Neco greet us as he enters the house. He is missing a finger, lost to a machine when he worked at a factory. El Chino Neco is a friend of my oldest brother. He is to be today's driver.

It is after Mamá lines up my little brothers to say goodbye to me. They have been awake since four o'clock or perhaps they, like my sisters and me, did not sleep at all. I hug them. Their bodies and faces give me the same feeling I get when I see withering flowers. I mourn their sadness, yet they stand at attention as though they are standing before the casket of someone quite important. It is just me, your sister who sometimes tickles you; the sister who bathes you under the mango tree and enjoys hearing you squeal as the cold water from the rain barrel falls on your skinny little bodies.

It is after Elvis asks halfway to the airport to let him out. He jumps from the pickup, and we continue, no goodbyes for him. I watch him shrink as we speed away, this long skinny twenty-five-year-old, a player of violins, the psychology student, who earns money playing piano at churches, who dresses in faded blue jeans, checkered shirts, and whose shadow might now be lost to me forever.

It is after the silent goodbyes that the real goodbyes at the airport in El Salvador begin. My mother's and sisters' sobs are partially blocked by my father's sad attempts to put on a brave face.

It is after I go inside my very first plane.

It is after I take my seat at a window, and imagine Mamá, Papá, my sisters, and my brother, in a row looking out at the big airplane, waiting to wave to me one last time. They too might be imagining me able to see them through these small windows, but I can't see much through the scratched Plexiglas. No one in my family has ever been in an airplane. I want to run out to them to tell them to come inside with me. As I try to get up, a stewardess stops me to tell me the restrooms are in the rear of the plane. As I try to go toward the front, another stewardess comes down the aisle ushering two little boys, one in each hand. They are dressed in black suits and are crying. She seats them both next to me. I feel it is too late. I start crying too, but in silence. I no longer know how to scream. I do not cry out. I touch their hands to console them.

The airplane starts moving. These kids are bawling. They seem no older than five and seven years old. The plane takes off. I feel as though I have swallowed seven buzzards. I want to vomit. I cannot see anything. I can only close my eyes. My lap is wet. These children pour their tears onto my lap.

It is after we arrive in Toronto and we are divided into groups. I feel like an animal in a zoo. They put us in some kind of fenced-in area so that we cannot get out. I learn that a Canadian family is adopting the two kids. In the zoo, the two boys are no longer with me, for they were culled into another group. I see the two children for the last time, as a tall white man with a nice face takes them away. He is holding their hands, pulling the kids along like two small coffins standing on end instead of lying flat. Everything seems a funeral in this moment. It is after the two boys look out to where I am and we signal our goodbyes, they with their eyes, I with a wave of my left hand. I am only capable of the weakest smile.

It is after the agents come to take away the different groups, that I realize I am not assigned to any group. I am left standing alone. Most of them are families or siblings traveling together. We are all exiles, but I am not with a family. There is one seemingly whole family, a Mamá, Papá, and two daughters, even a cousin whose family was killed. This family calls to the agents in Spanish to tell them to put me with them, so that I will go where they are going. As they lead away all the groups, I try to say something to an agent, but this agent has only come to take the family. He does not even acknowledge me, and leads the family away. The family looks appalled, as though they are being forced to leave behind a daughter, or something from their country that belongs to them or perhaps they think they belong to me. They call to me asking whether I am also being adopted. I say, "No."

"Where are you going?"

"I do not know. Canada," I say.

"Yes, you're in Canada, but where?"

"I do not know."

"You are too young to be on your own. We're going to Montreal. Tell the agent to send you there."

I am completely alone in the cage. I had learned from the two little boys that their parents and families were killed on the eastern side of El Salvador, and that, while looking for guerrillas, the soldiers had killed everyone older than twelve in their village. Across the country, wherever the military decimated the adult population, the children that were not taken by military officers to be adopted into their homes, were sent to refugee camps.

In my imagination Mamá, Papá, and my brother, and sisters are still lined up to stare at my airplane as it climbs into a sky of puffy white clouds. Or should I imagine them crying and wondering whether we will ever see each other again? Because of the collapse of languages filtering through my ears, the smell of some kind of food, perhaps bacon, pork, the clothes that people are wearing, I know I am thousands of kilometers away from my family, my people, my country. I feel ill at the thought of how far I am from Mamá, Papá, my sisters, brothers, aunts, from the roosters, chickens, and trees; from our dogs, and the dogs in the street; from the neighbors, even the ones we fought with, even the ones who were bad with me and with whom I was bad, and the good ones; from the little stores where I was sent to buy bread, eggs, and *queso con chile picoso*, (fake cheese); from the barrels filled with rainwater. I want to go home.

I see the morning sun, and Elvis' silhouette through foggy glass doors. I see the hills and the friends who went to hide in them. I see the Parque Libertad, and me waiting for Orlando, waiting, for the bus to go to the university to meet my friends. Now I miss the kids, the families who were in the plane with me. I miss my bed, my sisters and my brothers, but I think of my other brothers who went to Mexico with coyotes. I especially miss Mamá because I know she suffers for each of our journeys.

It is after the agent comes for me and asks me if I'm Dalai Iscamai..., a name I have never heard before, but when he shows me the written name, I say, "Yes." "Come." he says gesturing with his hand. I follow him. Then he explains very slowly, "You're going stay one night in Toronto. Wait for a person to take you to a hotel there. Tomorrow your final destination is Winnipeg, Manitoba. I shyly say, "Montreal?" He says, "No, Winnipeg." I insist, "Montreal?" "Do you understand what I'm saying? You're going to Winnipeg, not Montreal," he says firmly. Then he shows me the plane ticket. It says: final destination Winnipeg, Manitoba.

An agent takes me to a van, then to a hotel not far from Toronto airport. It is dark. I do not undress. I cannot sleep that night. I am afraid to be alone in the hotel room. I open the curtains and it is very bright. I have never seen so many electrical lights in my life. I stay there by the window until I hear people's noises and I finally fall asleep.

In the morning, I stand in front of the hotel waiting for a van to take me back to the airport. I follow other people going fast with suitcases. I concentrate on following them because I know we are going to wait together. I see shining floors, clean rust-colored carpeting, well-dressed tall people in cafes, so much light and electronic voices announcing something to confuse me. Everything is new, modern, and clean like the TV show I saw called "Miami Beach." The light is so white outside, and in front of me there's a garden of red, yellow, and pink tulips. Tulips! I have only seen them in magazines.

The immense sky is spotted with gigantic white clouds. A man comes to where I am waiting. His skin color looks like mine. His face resembles the faces of guys who dance in trances in *el parque* Libertad, the hari chrishnas. He says to me, "Winnipeg, no maletas? Vamos..." Before I am allowed to board the van he shows me my name on a list. He indicates for me to sign my name. I get in. There are other people in the van, who speak a language I don't understand. When I look around through the window from inside the van, I see there are many men like this driver, who are driving taxis and vans. At the airport someone takes us directly through to the airplane, finally through white clouds and some tears, I fall asleep.

It is after I arrive in Winnipeg, Manitoba, Canada, at two-thirty in the afternoon, or perhaps it is later or earlier. It is June 18, 1985. A woman waits for me, "Are you coming from El Salvador?" she asks in Spanish. "Si, soy yo," I respond. I have not been confused for anybody else. Whoever has been waiting here for me has found me. For a moment, my mother's face is her face. Sonya is the woman's name. She does not ask many questions, but explains things to me. "We're going to a hotel now. You're going to stay there for maybe a month, until we find you an apartment. I'll be your counselor at Manpower. Manpower will find you a school to learn English. At school you will make friends, and every two weeks you will pick up a check for food, clothes, and an apartment. When we find an apartment for you, I will take you there to show it to you and show you where to buy food and winter clothes. Tomorrow I'll take you to pick up some clothes for summer and fall.

You will be able to make one call to your family to tell them you have arrived, or you may write or send them a telegram if they do not have a phone. I just nod, and nod as she informs me about my new life. Her Spanish has an accent different from mine. I do not ask anything until she identifies herself as coming from Chile. "I have been living in Canada since 1975. I had to leave my family and country, too." Hearing that I feel a little better. I say thank you.

I am to be taken to the hotel with other immigrants in the van, but I am the only one who speaks Spanish. The van is very long, with a tall handsome guy in the back, explaining things in another language to three blond people who seem so white and tall. They're wearing black or brown leather jackets and nice blue jeans. They converse a lot with their counselor. I realize they are probably getting the same information Sonya gave me. Sonya is quiet, as I continue to be quiet, but I try to look through the van's window at this new place. Instead, I see Mamá, Papá, my sisters and brothers talking under the big mango tree in the light of a yolk-colored sunny sky. A group of young boys and girls walk by in sleeveless t-shirts, tight dark jeans...punks, with chains hanging from their pants, with spiked hair, and silver jewelry coming out their noses and through their lips. I am not sure why their look does not surprise me, except that I have seen some people like this on TV. But to see so many of them and in sleeveless shirts? The group breaks my family's image. In Toronto I felt cold, even though the sun was there.

" Is it cold outside?" I ask Sonya.

"The weather is very unstable. It's in summer here. Now it's very hot. Maybe we will have two more months like this before fall comes. Don't worry. We'll find you good boots and jackets."

" I brought these boots. My sisters bought them from a friend whose mother sent them from the USA. We spent the whole day before the trip looking for boots, but the only boots in El Salvador belong to the military. I was lucky she has the same size as me. I don't have other shoes. I just brought these boots I am wearing." I show her the brown thin fake leather boots under my blue jeans.

172

"Tomorrow I'll take you to find some shoes for walking."

"Thank you." I realize I've never used this expression so much as in these last few moments' conversation. Sonya never says "you're welcome" or de nada. She just pats me on the leg.

"I should have read about the seasons in Canada. These boots are hot. And I can't walk well in them. I thought it was always winter here. I bought a magazine in El Salvador that said it is always cold in Canada." I took out the old 1970s magazine that says something about the secrets of Calgary's mountains.

"It's usually colder, but today, it's hot." She smiles for the first time since the airport.

She brings me to a hotel named Marlborough. I feel somehow set apart from the others, and I wish my family and my friends were here. It is a nice hotel... not new, but nice. It looks like something from a movie. The other people are getting out of the van, and happily kissing the cheeks of their counselor. Sonya tells me that they are Polish immigrants coming from a refugee settlement in Italy. This surprises me, although I do not know anything about Poland, other than that the Pope who visited El Salvador to honor Monseñor Romero is from Poland. My friends and I, we think he is full of shit and he is a right-winger. Poland! Isn't that close to Russia? Russia is our dream society in El Salvador, well, not for all Salvadorans.

Sonya gives more information about what to expect from the refugee settlement program. "We'll see you tomorrow." She gets a key for me and tells me I will be in room number 205. I look at the dark brown carpet, and beige walls of the lobby. I go upstairs. The long halls are like the boulevards we just drove through to get here. People stand by the doors of their rooms. They are staring at me. I step quickly into room number 205.

It is after I carry a false passport and a warmly striped bag of woven Guatemalan colors inside the hotel room. I finally open the soft Guatemalan bag. The first thing I remove is an old National Geographic magazine I bought at a stand for used books on the street in San Salvador the day before I left. On the cover are the mountains of Calgary I showed Sonya in the van. I know I need to read something, anything that can help me to understand this unknown land at journey's end. From the soft Guatemalan bag I pull a pair of extra pants, a pair of underwear

173

and a bra. I find a bag with hard cheese inside. "In case you are hungry in the plane," Mamá said at the airport.

It is after I walk toward the tall square window. I am holding the photo Mamá put in my pocket. In it we are all ten years younger. I turn it over and it says on the back in my mother's handwriting, "Te queremos." I look through the window at the empty streets. Even though it looks to be only four o'clock in the afternoon, there are no pedestrians in sight. I press my face as high as I can reach against the pane of glass to look down to the street below. The buildings seems so cold, so strangely cold, and so impersonal. Reddish-brown brick buildings are everywhere, I can't see any mountains. I wonder where the mountains of Calgary are. I want to see the San Salvador volcano I see from the terrace of the unfinished mansion.

It is after I walk toward the bed.

It is after I sit on it. and turn on the TV. All the talk from that box is noise. I stare at the mouths of the people. I don't know how to change the channels. I do not understand what they are saying. It makes me want to sleep. It is summer, and I wonder why I feel cold.

It is after the TV is still flickering. I can understand the numbers. It is seven o'clock. It is morning. Sunlight streams down through an overcast sky. I know I am in a new land, but the world I see is still my homeland, the place where I know who I am. Only after this do the tears flow so strong that I feel I might drown myself in my tears forever.

Glossary of Foreign Terms

Antiguo Cuscatlán- a municipality in the La Libertad department of El Salvador, and it is also part of the Metropolitan Area of San Salvador.
Cuzcatlan- one of the Province of El Salvador. Also The Lordship of Cuzcatlán, was a pre- colonial Nahuat nation . Now El Salvador.
abuela- grandmother
amate - a kind of large tree; Amate Marin- the name of a place
bisabuela- great grandmother
barranca- a gully
bule, bule- a 1960's Rock song
buenos días- good morning
burdeles- house of prostitution
buenas tarde- good afternoon
brujo- sorcerer
cabrones – dumbass/ bastard
cadejo negro- black magic dog (Legend Salvadoran Character)
canela- cinnamon
cántaro- plastic jug
cafetales- coffee plantation
camándulas- the Rosary
colonia –residential/ neighborhood
comal-thin disk of unglazed earthenware or metal used for cooking tortillas, roasting coffee or cocoa, or grill any type of food.
chile- hot chile spiced powder put on green mangoes

cuartel zapote- zapote barracks/ headquarter military
espiritu de caña- alcoholic cheap brand
mercado cuartel- ex -Barrack craft market
colonos- Work for someone who owns coffee plantations and give the person or the family a small place, a garden like piece of land to grown vegetables, tokens to buy food, clothes, usually in the owner's store some and all the family has to work for them. The can leave if they want. Sharecroppers.
cantarito de barro- clay jug- a sweet nickname
caserios- farmhouses for workers- hamlet
canton- a small town or village or even a rural
chicha- alcoholic drinks, which are produced mainly based on non- distilled fermented corn and pineapple peel,husk, and other fruits .
cinconegrito-Shrub in the family of the Verbenáceas, with aromatic leaves and flowers. Medicinal plant.
cipitio -is the child of the Siguanaba. (Legend -Salvadoran Character)
comadre- godmother
corazón de Jesús- heart of Jesus/ image
doña- middle-aged or old Lady
El Mozote – 1. Plant- 2.- Name of a place-El Mozote Massacre took place in and around the village of El Mozote, in Morazán department, El Salvador, on December 11, 1981,when the Salvadorian Army killed more than 800 civilians. El Salvador Del Mundo- The Salvadoran Saver Saint
epazote – Plant/medicinal herb
fincas -refers to a piece of rural or agricultural land
derechista- right –wing
dulce - sweet
hola- hello
hija- daughter
hombre-man
hermano-brother

hijo de puta- son of a bitch
indios- indigenous people/ in this case anyone mestizo but from the countryside.
Jardines de guadalupe/ a middle class neighborhood
LP 28- student movement organization(leftist)
Fapu- student movement organization
maquilisguat-The national tree of El Salvador. Pink flowers.
maiz- Corn
mercado - public Market
mesón- a kind of hostel but family live in these mesones.
mona negra- black little female monkey/ nickname for a little girl n the book.
muñeco- male doll- in this case is an alcoholic brand.
mundo de juguetes- world of toys- 1970's Mexican Soap-opera
monseñor- archbishop
morro- a fruit tree where its seeds are use to make horchata drink, and containers like a cup.
muchachos- young boys- in this context guerrillas.
Nahuat- Indigenous Language in El Salvador
niña- Little Girl
Niño de Atocha – Holly child of Atocha
gente maldita- damn people
orejas- Snipers
panela de dulce - Sugar cane
paletas- Popsicles
parabienes – songs chant in children funerals mostly in poor people houses.
Parque Libertad- Main park or plaza in down town San Salvador
patron - owner of a coffee plantation/ boss
Pantorrilas rellenitas – solid calves
pobre- poor use as in compassion
Puerto de Acajutla- Port of Acajutla is outside the capital of San Salvador. In Sonsonate.

ranchera- traditional music of Mexico
salones de baile- Dance halls or ballroom
Sonsonate- one of the fourteen departments in El Salvador.
Santa Ana – one of the departments in El Salvador.
La Siguanaba- is a well-known figure from both
Salvadoran and Guatemalan mythology. She was originally
called Sihuehuet, which means beautiful woman, when she
had an affair with the son of god, Tlaloc and became
pregnant. However, she was an irresponsible mother and
left her young son alone while she satisfied her desires.
subversivos – anyone who is against the government.
tatarabuela- great great grandmother
tatita- another way of calling a grandfather
tecomate – gourd- in one time use to carry water for
peasants.
Torta- egg yolk bread in a shape of rock
tía/ tío- aunt/ uncle
tombilla- straw basket for clothes
Tres Ceibas- 1. ceiba name of a large tropical tree. And
the name of a place.
 Sunza- a tropical fruit.

About the Author

Carolina Rivera Escamilla is a writer, performer and filmmaker. Born in El Salvador, she was granted political asylum in Canada in 1985. Four years later, as the Berlin Wall fell and the guerillas of El Salvador made their final offensive; Carolina joined the massive immigration of Salvadorans to Los Angeles so she could be more involved with the culture and politics of her community. She completed her undergraduate degree in English Literature with an emphasis in Creative Writing at University of California, Los Angeles. A Fellow in the PEN USA Rosenthal Foundation's Emerging Voices Program, her story *The Funeral* was included in *Strange Cargo*, a Pen Emerging Voices Anthology. Director, writer, and producer of the documentary: *Manlio Argueta, Poets and Volcanoes*.

www.carolinariveraescamilla.com